HELL'S DOORSTEP

Also by David P. Holmes

Fiction:
Secrets
Emily's Run
Loose Gravel
HellBurger

Non fiction:
Salt of the Earth

Contact with the author is welcome through his website
www.davidpaulholmes.com

HELL'S DOORSTEP

David P. Holmes

NORTH STAR PRESS OF ST. CLOUD, INC.

Saint Cloud, Minnesota

First Edition: June 2013

Printed in the United States of America

Published by
North Star Press of St. Cloud, Inc.
P.O. Box 451
St. Cloud, Minnesota 56302

www.northstarpress.com | Facebook - North Star Press | Twitter - North Star Press

"Dying is easy. You have to fight to live."
Eddie Rickenbacker

CHAPTER ONE

● ●

Duluth, Minnesota, 1:00 a.m., June. Hell Burger Restaurant.

"HEY, PAPPY, SLIP US A COUPLE FOR THE LAST CALL." I laid a twenty on the counter as an incentive, and it worked.

"Sure thing, Norby. Then you and the princess gotta get out. I'm gonna have my hands full with the boss. He's feeling his cups again."

Mitch Omer, one of the owners of Hell Burger, my hangout in Duluth, was dancing on a table top, sloshing a glass of red wine in his hand. His wife, Cynthia Gerdes, sat quietly at a corner table waiting to pick up the pieces. No, I don't know why they have different last names. It never mattered.

I had a Windsor Pepsi and handed Angie two inches of bar booze. She was a better man than I was. We ceremoniously clinked our glasses, "Cheers." She was a bar fly that had passed her prime a decade ago, but she was still a beautiful woman, if you looked deep enough. She was the kind of drunk that had a metabolism that turned booze to skinny. Long scraggily dark-blonde hair battled with the encroaching gray and did whatever it wanted on the top of her head. Her face hadn't seen make-up, or soap, for quite a while. The flesh that covered her frame just kind of hung loosely, holding her inner parts in place. Her manner of clothing could best be described as generic. Whatever was on top of the laundry pile was what adorned her body. Underwear was an option. If she'd ever gone to school, it hadn't been for very long. The need to earn a living to support all the men attached to her was job number one. That and a serious coke habit of her own. At age ten her stepfather introduced her to an insidious game of perversion to quell his addiction. At twelve she found that men would pay for sex, thus pushing her education in a different direction. As she aged, and the abortions, drugs, abuse, and liquor took a toll on her body, she became what she currently was. In spite of

1

what life had done to her, she was still a nice person. That scored big in my book. Just the fact that she'd consider talking to me was a plus.

Tonight, the guy she was living with was on another rampage looking for an easy target to punch. That was usually her, but she saw the warning signs soon enough this time and split. She had negotiated a safe warm place to sleep tonight, with me, in exchange for carnal pleasures and copious amounts of alcohol. She tossed her drink down her throat, shook her head, and rasped, "Ahrrrg." I took that as an endearing comment meaning she was ready to go. Myself, I was never smart enough to leave before I got tossed out.

Moving to the door, I waved goodbye to Cynthia and watched Mitch go tea-pot off the table. She shook her head and dutifully went in to repair the damage.

The outside lights to Hell Burger had been shut off, giving the garish façade in front an eerie glow cast by the parking lot security lamps. Angie was working on the words she wanted to form, coming up with, "Your place now? You better get me to bed before I pass out. I'm a lousy lay when I'm asleep." She burped.

Enamored with her feminine attributes, I tended to look upon her little characteristics as cute. I had to or I'd go home alone.

She was leaning in to me to seal the deal with a kiss when I heard the splat and her face exploded.

Bone, brain matter, blood, and flesh stung my face while I stared at the open pink of the remaining part of her head. The body fell back and clumped to the pavement. My brain came out of hiding, and I screamed. The moment I fell to my knees, I felt the next slug whiz past my own face and slam into the gaudy display that was the front of Hell Burger.

Cranking my head over my shoulder I caught the taillights of a car as it slowly moved away on Canal Park Drive, in no obvious hurry.

I don't know when I stopped screaming. My next moment of consciousness was realizing I was sitting in the back seat of a cop car, my legs out the door and my head either up my ass or between my knees. There was a pile of barf between my feet. Looking up, I saw the blurred image of my friend, Detective Lieutenant Stu Grosslein. His concern for my condition was welcome as he screeched at me, "What the hell did you do, Klein?"

I felt the drool dripping down my chin and slobbered the words, "Angie, Stu. It was Angie. It just . . . just." I didn't know how to say anything else. Time had braked to a sudden stop, dropping me into a terrifying place. As vacant as my comprehension was, the truth was clear as good vodka. Angie's murder was a message, and the second slug was the exclamation mark. Her death was intentional and I was missed on purpose.

Psycho-bitch was back and her game had begun.

CHAPTER TWO

● ● ● ● ● ● ● ● ● ● ● ● ● ● ● ● ● ● ● ●

Mʏ ɴᴀᴍᴇ ɪs Nᴏʀʙᴇʀᴛ Kʟᴇɪɴ ʙᴜᴛ I ᴘʀᴇꜰᴇʀ to be called Norby. I was named after an alcoholic uncle whom my parents thought would be impressed and leave them his fortune. Instead, he drank up his bank account, only leaving me a stupid name. Once, before he died of scleroses, he called me a little snot and told me I was a mistake and my parents didn't love me. Yeah, so?

I cringe when I hear the rhythmic bass of Johnny Cash signing, "A boy named Sue." My mind translates the lyric into, "A dope named Norbert."

All through school my friends thought my name was Chuck. Lying was easier and safer than fighting.

Today, I'm a private eye and my business is rounding up bad guys, snooping on cheaters, serving subpoenas to people who don't want them—all while trying to avoid being arrested myself. I've been on the hard end of a nightstick a few times, and I enjoyed the ambience of our local house of correction on occasion. But only when I wasn't able to lie my way out of it.

If anyone needed to find me, it helped if they were a young attractive babe. I avoid the rest of everyone else as much as possible. Locating me shouldn't be too difficult. I can usually be found hanging onto the bar at my favorite haunt, the Hell Burger Restaurant, in the Canal Park area of Duluth. It's the Duluth in Minnesota, not Georgia. Who'd ever go to Georgia? I stay in this Duluth to enjoy freezing for twelve months.

At Hell Burger, I've got a spot at the end of the bar where I can lean against the wall so I don't fall down. I keep a bunch of those yellow sticky note things stuck to the wall at my end of the bar. I call them FLYN's. That's an acronym for Friggin' Little Yellow Notes.

I've pissed off a good number of people, and serving subpoenas is a catalyst for just that. Cheating husbands, jealous husbands, prowling housewives, dirty cops—at one time or another they all vowed to bring an end to my life. This time, however, I think the pledge to end my life is real. There's a deranged woman prowling the streets of Duluth with plans to kill me.

I've put myself out there as bait hoping the queen-of-unhinged-minds would bite, but other than a few close calls, she's managed to elude me. The last time I saw her close up, she was sitting on my chest about to cut my throat with a large knife. When her mother planted a bullet into her back, it just ruined all her plans to kill me. When the police finally showed up, all that was left of her was a trail of blood.

I got involved with Kathleen Pierpont, Miss El-Strange-o, in my last gig. To make a sordid story short, her mother hired me to locate her cheating husband and a fortune in bearer bonds. I found the guy, getting my first glimpse of his naked bulbous body in the trunk of a stolen Cadillac. His last human experience in life was on top of a prostitute who wound up with the bonds after she helped kill him. Not being in full control of my libido, I naturally fell in love with the hooker and almost died for it—twice.

I eventually found the bearer bonds and put some of them to good use. The rest are someplace else, and that's as much as I'll say on that. When rich people are enticed with getting richer, they get mean and hurt the simple folks who get in the way. I'd like to stop that from happening, and I have no delusion about getting my throat slit or having a 9 mil run up my butt.

Today, I'm trying to give the impression I'm penniless, but what's the point of having money if you don't spend it? Or, drink it? Or give it to lovely ladies with special talents? Okay, I'm weak. Mitch Omer and Cynthia Gerdes, owners of my second home, Hell Burger, have welcomed me with open arms—as long as I was spending. Cynthia was by far more compassionate than Mitch, merely screaming at me to get out of the bar, as opposed to Mitch physically tossing me out. Once, he chased me through Canal Park with a meat cleaver but gave up when he forgot what he was running for. I thought it was a flash-back from the sixties snapping his mind into a different era. A more fun one.

My biggest catch of the Pierpont case was discovering that the cheating husband's mistress, the lovely and deadly Kathleen Pierpont, was his own daughter, a willing accomplice, aptly named psycho-bitch. Yup, same one. This vixen had a sex drive that should have been outlawed. Yes, of course I sampled it. If you saw her you would too. On the not so bright side, this babe was also a murdering, conniving, manipulating maiden that let nothing stand in her way. Until she met me. I put a stop to her game, and after two attempts to murder me, she skipped town. Maybe psycho-bitch is too mild of a term to fully comprehend the evil that pushes her. Godzilla meets Hitler.

Right now I was sitting in the office of a shrink who was trying to help me find myself. I wasn't lost, I was here. I didn't want to be here. I was forced to do this. If she wasn't such a babe, I'd find it easier to leave. The reason I was here today, other than the prompting by the chief of police, was that I thought Kathleen Pierpont was getting closer, wanting nothing less than the satisfaction of slitting my throat. It had me kind of nervous. Maybe scared shitless would cover it. The cops didn't want me dead until they found out where I hid the remaining bearer bonds.

I used to have a thriving business in a swank suburb of Minneapolis, but got too involved with my client. After a downhill trip, I landed in Duluth. Things were better now, except for the psychotic sex maniac bent on seeing me dead. Man, I really pissed her off.

Back in the shrink's office, the inquisition was about to begin, and I had to strain to be able to hear her. I'd rather sit and look at her, feeling more like Tony Soprano visiting his shrink. She was sitting about two inches from me, her legs crossed so that I could follow the line of flesh up through her skirt to her playground. The heat coming from her would melt the ice in a hockey arena.

Her voice was soft and as disturbing as the open gap in her skirt where those two marvelous weapons of mass destruction were crossed. The diplomas adorning the walls confirmed she was a real psychiatrist, but she didn't learn this seduction act studying the *Handbook of Psychiatric Measures*. If she had I was going to get a copy.

She sets a recorder on the small table next to her, pressing the button. "Do you mind if I record this?"

"Do I have a choice?"

"No. Shall we begin?"

I had to lean forward so she wouldn't see my physical reaction to her legs. "Ask away, Doc."

"Mr. Klein, we've already addressed the terms of identity. I'm to be called Dr. LaRioux, and you are, of course, Mr. Klein. That is for the purpose of identity so there can never be any contradiction. Understand?" Her voice was soft and I was trying to recognize her plea for me to take her to bed.

"You said nobody will ever hear what I say."

Why did she have to pout her lips when she talked? "That's correct."

I was trying to not be an ass, but I was curious, "If nobody will ever hear this, and it's just you and me, why so formal? Can't we just be Ariel and Norby?"

The pout turned to a sneer. "Let's get on with this. Do you know why this woman you refer to as, uhm, psycho-bitch, wants to kill you? Do you mind if we refer to her as Ms Pierpont? Hmm?"

Duh. "I broke up her operation and stole millions of dollars from her."

"Aren't the police looking into it?"

Another duh. "The only thing they're going to look into is the hole in my head from a large caliber bullet. Or my severed head."

"Why do you refer to her, as you put it, a psychotic sex maniac? At one time her family was a stanchion of society. I'd like to keep our discussions on a more professional level."

"She wouldn't stop screwing me. Look at me. I'm a slob, and every time I looked at her, she got undressed. She was boinking her own father and maybe the rest of Duluth. To me, that spells psychotic sex maniac."

"You mean Ms Pierpont."

Duh again. "Yeah."

"Maybe she was attracted to you."

How many duh's was this going to take? "No, she was attracted to my finding her goddamn money."

Her eyebrows went up, generating the next question. "My understanding is that there were millions in those bonds. What happened to all of it?" She leaned forward to facilitate her blouse opening ever so slightly. Maybe she was showing off the lacy bra I was entitled to glimpse. In a world of reality, it was a gesture to capture my revealing the location of the bonds.

Now I was being pumped. Her goal in talking to me was to divulge where I've stashed all that money. "Well, as you've already read in the police report, the hooker that helped kill the philanderer stole the bonds. Then she turned about half the bonds into cash. The philanderer's daughter, Ms Pierpont as you insist, who also helped the hooker kill him—her father—stole the cash from the hooker. Still with me on this? The hooker then, as you have also read in the police report, absconded with the remaining bonds, and she was murdered for it. But, the hooker hid the bonds. You know all that. Why ask me again?"

Ignoring me, she asked her own questions. "Let me get this straight. You say the daughter stole the cash, and is now trying to kill you. If she has the cash, why would she bother with you?"

"The bonds were originally given to the philandering asshole by an Arab splinter group to buy weapons in this country. To keep the Arabs from coming down on the family, they turned the cash over to them, mortgaged the mansion for the rest, and that's when psy— ... excuse me, Ms Pierpont, tried to do me in. She was royally pissed."

Those lips parted again but instead of rubbing them on my face as I had been hoping, she started asking more dumb questions. "The prostitute hid the bonds. You found them, didn't you?"

Nice try, lady. I sat staring at her legs, wondering how far my hand would get before she'd stop me. My ogling caused her to take the next step, much to my relief. She folded her notebook, straightened her skirt, and told me in a soft voice I strained to hear, "That'll be all for our first session, Mr. Klein. Please come back next week and we can continue."

She handed me a card with the day and time I was supposed to come back and lie on her couch. If she was under, or on top me, it didn't matter which, I could see a reason for showing up. For a shrink, she was one awesome babe, but she ran charge water through her veins.

Glad to get out of her office, the door shut behind me. I turned back and scoffed at the name on the door, Ariel LaRioux, psychiatrist. I'd bet a pint of Old Mister Boston she paid her way through med school on her back. Well, the thought was enticing.

I tossed the card and stood on the busy Duluth street wondering where I had parked my car. I turned east, and after three blocks, remembered I should have turned west. I might be an idiot, but I was a respectable one. At least I had a job. Sort of.

When I took on the case to find the bearer bonds and make love to the psychotic sex maniac, I had an office in the Miller Hill area. My secretary, Kung Foo Jeanine, was paying her own salary and the bills from her savings account. After my retainer from Adelle Pierpont, the rich wife of the naked bulbous guy screwing his daughter, Jeanine decided to keep the business afloat and reimburse her savings. Much to my surprise, and relief, she took over the business, hiring an Amazon called Bruin Heinz, to replace me.

Jeanine always ran the business anyway. She knew where the staples were kept, just what size trash can liner to use, and the account number to our overdrawn bank account. Nobody stayed in business without having a Jeanine to take care of it. I liked having her around if I ran out of paper clips, and she was drop dead centerfold gorgeous. Aside from the tight shape, perfect set of hoo-hoos, a butt that was actually round, and the long blonde ponytail, there was more. She could fire a softball that slowed down to ninety-five miles per hour by the time it got over the plate, was an expert shot with anything that spit out bullets, could kick Jackie Chan from here to Tuesday while beating the hell out of Chuck Norris, and she scared the beejeebers out of me.

As for my Amazonic lesbian replacement, Brew could cook a Pop Tart in her armpit, and put Colonel Steve Austin, that bionic million-dollar guy, out to pasture. I won't go into my fear of how she might cook hot dogs. I'd never seen her do it, but there was a rumor that she lifted weights with her lips.

I might be an idiot, yes, I'd already established that, but I was smart enough to avoid confronting a six-foot-three lesbian that lifted weights and ate hot rivets in malt liquor. I learned early on that if I didn't use her preferred name of "Brew," I'd be welded into my Plymouth Reliant and tossed into the compactor.

My name was still on the letterhead, and I had a small table in the rear of the office to set my coffee cup on. Jeanine and Brew had nice walnut desks with shiny tops and lots of office gadgets to adorn them. While Jeanine and Brew were in the conference room making out, I stole their paper clips. Brew was an out-and-out confirmed lesbian, but I knew for fact Kung Foo Jeanine was hetero. But selective with whom she shared her treats. I put the make on her once. Wound up in the hospital.

When I had the office, I never bothered attaching a name to it, simply listed in the yellow pages as, Norby Klein, Private Investigator. Now the girls had a half page add with the new name embarrassingly emblazoned over it: Pink Power Investigations. The front window boasted more estrogen pumping supremacy with huge pink letters blocking my view of the girls walking into Starbucks.

The main source of income for the pink investigators came from women locating cheating husbands, women looking for favorable evidence in divorce cases, women looking for alibis on their own indiscretions, and women looking for a way to make life miserable for men. I was still confused over this weaker sex concept. Occasionally, I'd be handed a case like finding out if the junk yard dog really bit the bum who broke in to sleep in an old mini-van.

When I was turned away from Hell Burger, I walked home to my apartment on Superior Street, not far from Canal Park. My section of Superior Street was like the hovel that sat outside the castle walls, far enough away to not spoil the idleness of the affluent.

On balmy summer days and evenings, the Canal Park section of Duluth was bustling with young girls from the college, and young guys from the college, trolling for a hit. Tanned bodies clad in khaki shorts and tank tops, hidden behind Ray Bans, cavorting from one bar to the next, volleyed for position in the never ending game of pick-up.

If I stumbled home in the dark I was usually certain I'd get a visit from my good friend Hankie. I didn't know, and didn't want to know, his last name, but I called him Hankie because his first name was Homer. Clever huh? Hankie had never heard of the Twins or even seen a baseball game. And as long as I kept him supplied in Mad Dog and Silver Satin, he was willing to let himself be my friend.

Hankie let it slip once that he came from a high level job out East and held a Masters degree. I think he's a lawyer, but I won't hold that against him. My gut told me he killed his wife and now hid in the sewers of Duluth.

I know that some day his arteries would turn into soda straws, and he needed more than alcohol to survive, but I couldn't bring myself to try changing him. Occasionally, when the street filled with cop cars looking for whatever, I'd hide Hankie in my apartment. Unfortunately, he's infested it with lice.

Hankie was more than a friend I kept buying cheap wine for. He was my eyes in the neighborhood. I needed him to tell me what was going on in the darkness of his world that was too despicable to be allowed in daylight. A few weeks ago when he told me about a tall, slender shadow creeping around the abandoned appliance store that housed my apartment, I immediately thought of Kathleen Pierpont, returning for vengeance. Her money was gone, so all she could do was satisfy a psychotic need to kill me. Or anyone standing close to me. Killing Angie in front of Hell Burger was the start of her game, and I feared she was going to draw it out as long as it tickled her.

Being an industrious hard-working sort, I had a second job. Sort of. After busting the Pierpont case wide open, the Duluth chief of police offered me a job as a consultant with the Duluth Precinct on West First Street. Much to the chagrin of my lifelong friend and fellow police force member Lieutenant Stu Grosslein, I was made an honorary member of his fraternity. It was a no-brainer to me that the chief made the offer to keep me close and under observation. They wanted to know where the missing bonds had gone to, and how, so suddenly, so many charitable organizations had become fluent with large bank accounts.

My answer, "A good Samaritan?" to the chief's question was received with skepticism. And to further his discomfort, Detective Stu Grosslein was given orders to baby sit me until the bonds showed up. Then, after I was in jail for embezzlement, they could get on with their lives as donut jockeys in Dunn Bros.

There was another twist in the story. The bearer bonds originated with a radical from Afghanistan or Iran, or who cares, wanting to buy weapons through ex-ambassador Elwood Pierpont. Unfortunately, his daughter's sex drive and my helping her satisfy it, got in the way. Now, I might have not only the psychotic sex maniac after me, but a few geopolitical misfits. Also, Kathleen Pierpont ran something called "The Syndicate" as a strong-arm enforcer to her operation. Being a resourceful psychotic sex maniac, she ran a prostitution ring to add to the charm of the whole thing. When her main screw, Laura Blake, stole the bonds and talked me into helping her, it started the decline of the empire.

To make a sordid story short, I had a murderous bitch, a fanatical Mideast underworld, the remnants of the mysterious syndicate, and a disgruntled pimp all wanting me dead. So, I was told by the chief of police that I was going to see the precinct psychiatrist to ease my woes. At some point they were going to hypnotize me and pull out my fingernails to get some answers. If the shrink knew how easily she could get it done by sitting on my face I'd be in the sewer with Hanky very quickly.

CHAPTER
THREE

● ● ● ● ● ● ● ● ● ● ● ● ● ● ● ● ● ● ●

I WASN'T IN THE MOOD TO FACE KUNG FOO JEANINE and her muscle, Brew, so I dropped into the police station to see if there was a pay check waiting for me. I didn't have a desk there either, so I hung out in Grossy's office. There was a coffee pot in the squad room, and since I favored coffee that tastes like an enema, I made myself welcome.

The traffic in the police station was minimal, with a handful of uniforms jawing about a possible geriatric Brett Favre comeback. Two more plainclothes were slouched over crossword puzzles or scouting porn on the computer. My eyes were on heat-seeking mode and spied my target. I meandered over to the nearest desk to share wisdom and war stories with Loretta Thielges, a tiny sweet blonde gal that sat there day after day pounding out reports on a typewriter. I plunked down next to her desk and a ray of sunshine came from a broad, beaming smile. "Hi, Norby. What brings you to our part of hell?"

"Hi, twerp. I just dropped in to see if there was any work for the department's only paid consultant. And, of course, to flirt with you."

She reached out to touch my arm, singing, "Why you old sweetie you."

Old?

Pulling open her desk drawer, she handed me an envelope. "Pay day, Norbs."

Oh, my God, a check. I ripped it open to gaze in wonder at the one hundred dollar figure. "Loretta, you have made me the happiest man on earth."

"And I didn't even have to sleep with you."

I handed the check back to her, asking, "Is this enough?"

She had a way of laughing that lit up my life. As she rolled with joy, her long ponytail swung, making her look like a homecoming queen. The blue in those large eyes was absolutely clear enough to be able to see down to her soul. The happy frolicking wasn't going to last, I knew. I saw my friend Detective Lieutenant

Stu Grosslein stomp into his office, steam rolling from his puffy face. Through the glass partition, Loretta and I stiffened as he bellowed, "Klein, Thielges, get in here."

Loretta's little body shot out of the chair and came to attention. "He's not happy."

"Well, I'm not either, but I'm not going to scream about it."

"Let's see what he wants." Holding her utility belt from rattling, she led me into Detective Grosslein's inner sanctum chamber.

"Close the door. Sit down." There was only one chair, and Loretta beat me to it. I was still holding my cup of enema.

"Klein, your about to earn your keep for a change." Getting straight to business, he told Loretta, "Thielges, you take this mess with you," nodding to me, "and check out a dead body they found out by the old water plant on London Road."

He looked at me, trying to scowl, and I had to hold back my grin at his theatrics.

"You sober today, Klein?"

"I don't know, Grossy. I can't tell the difference anymore."

The steam shooting from his nostrils was real. "The chief needs to attach some hours to your existence here to justify those paychecks. Go with Officer Thielges and come back to make a report."

Man, I'd love to be the paper salesman for this place.

Officer Thielges, who carried the nickname Rikki, was bubbling with excitement. At last, she was going to be a real cop. Her utility belt held handcuffs, a flashlight, a real gun which probably even had a bullet in it, and some pouches, probably for make up and condoms. Dancing out of the precinct house, she was giddy like a kid on Christmas. "C'mon, Norby, we can check out a patrol car."

Running after her, I called out, "Can we turn on the lights and siren? Huh? Please?" She consented to the lights but thought the siren went against some department policy.

A police car was a war wagon. Equipped with a computer, fax machine, life saving gadgets, an arsenal of weapons, cameras, radar, more lights than a Christmas tree, Kevlar armor in the doors, and a siren that Rikki won't let me use. There was a power plant under the hood that could launch this baby to the moon, housing the typical Crown-Vic, P71 with a supercharged 4.6 L V8, four-speed. Especially exciting to me—this time I was sitting up front, not shackled in the back seat.

She turned the key and I pretended I was in the cockpit of an F-35. Man.

Rikki moved the machine into traffic, flipped on the red-and-blue lights, and I hung on for dear life. My petite little girl was a lead-foot.

At the east end of London Road, sitting at the edge of Kitchi-gummi, known as Lake Superior to the lesser informed, where Highway 61 stretched north to Canada, sat the old water treatment plant. Built in 1897 the damn thing kept pumping twenty-million gallons of Lake Superior into Duluth, every day. Considered a historical site by some society bent on preservation, today it became a crime scene.

Bouncing over the curb, she ran the patrol car into the yellow barrier tape. Rikki bolted out before the car's engine was dead. Trying to stem her eagerness, I cautioned her, "Rikki, slow down. The stiff's not going anywhere."

Like a kid going to the circus, she turned and hissed, "C'mon, Norby. Get your ass out here. I don't want to go in there by myself." She nervously eyed the two cops staring at us.

This being her first real assignment in her three-year stint on the force, I could understand her being apprehensive. I just wanted to be sure she looked professional to the seasoned cops standing by the body, leering at her. At her butt, really.

Stepping under the tape with her, I tried to calm her down. "Easy, girl, just be natural with these guys." She was about to step into a good-old-boy's club with a strict code of tenure before any acceptance was granted. Especially to a rookie. And even a tougher hurdle, a female.

The first cop we encountered was a thirty-year veteran leaning against a tree with his thumbs hooked in his belt. His comment didn't make Rikki feel any better. "Well, if it isn't Beavis and Butthead. Out to play cop for a while?"

I knew this beast, having been on the hard end of his night stick a few times. He had the pleasure of busting and cuffing me more than once. He stepped forward holding his beefy mitt out to stop me. "That's far enough, Klein. Real cops only here. Move back to the tape."

I pulled out my complimentary badge and flashed it to him. "I am a cop, Bozo. I'm assisting Officer Thielges under orders from Lieutenant Grosslein. You want to argue with him, go ahead. You need to be put out to pasture anyway. Before you get bumped for interfering, I gotta ask, did you bag any evidence? Take pictures? Question witnesses? Pick your nose? Scratch your ass? If not, get out of our way and go do it."

I watched the second officer standing aside thinking it was smarter to do just that. Rikki and I slowly circled the body looking for anything obvious. So the other cop wouldn't hear, I quietly said, "Honey, go get the camera and evidence bags."

Catching on, she nodded and left. I stayed back wanting Rikki to get credit for everything. I knew the stiff sprawled over the lawn, and was glad he was dead. Otherwise, he'd be up trying to kill me—again.

Rikki trotted back and set the satchel on the grass. I just knew her mind raced through the procedures manual trying to recall the basics for a crime scene examination. I watched as that marvelous organ in her head clicked her into action like a seasoned professional. She set about taking pictures and bagging anything that might be evidence. The next step was to determine if this was a homicide, suicide, accident, or death by natural causes. Turning the body over, I let Rikki decide that the red hole in the back of his head indicated the guy was murdered. Execution. I went back to the patrol car to radio for the CSI unit. Yeah, there really was a thing like that in real life. I was never lucky enough to meet Marg Helgenberger, but maybe, someday.

Off the horn to the station, I met up with Officer Beast. His real name was Darrel Snerd, and he had taken enough abuse through the years for it, so I left the insults alone. His thumbs permanently imbedded, hooked into his belt, stayed where they were. Eyeing Officer Thielges, bent over the body, Officer Snerd couldn't keep his mouth shut. "Man, I'd like to get into her pants."

I glanced at his target and couldn't blame him for wanting to, but defended Rikki's honor, "You might as well, Snerd, there's one asshole in there already."

His retort, less than civilized, "Fuck you, Klein."

Smiling at his discomfort, I told him, "Watch for the forensics crew, okay?" I got another nasty remark from him, but knew he'd do it.

Back at the body, I asked, "Any ID?"

"No, he's clean. Maybe the lab will find something." She saw my interest in the dead guy and was bright enough to ask, "You know him, Norby?"

I didn't want to answer her. I wanted to walk away and never look back. I wanted this scene to be different. Once this can of worms was opened I'd be on the hot seat with Grosslein again. I shook off the spell holding me there and answered her. "Yeah, I know him. A couple years ago I thought I killed him."

I explained to Officer Thielges, "He was one of a bunch of guys staked out at my apartment waiting for me." I kept the rest of the story from her for my own reason. It was too painful to talk about. While I was launching a 9 mil into this guy, Psycho-bitch was upstairs in my apartment slicing the throat of the prostitute who stole the bonds. On my bed.

CHAPTER
FOUR

● ●

I WAITED IN THE PATROL CAR WHILE OFFICER THIELGES worked with the medical examiner, handing over the evidence bags and the camera. About an hour later, the stiff was bagged and loaded in the meat wagon. No need for lights and sirens now.

I was startled by the sight of my friend once she was back behind the wheel of the unit. Rikki's fingers pinched the key in the ignition, but she didn't turn it. She looked so small and frail dressed in a grown-up outfit designed to protect her life and enforce the law. The garbage hanging on her belt was lethal, and with her training, so was she. However, what the girl I saw should have been dancing through the mall with her friends laughing and giggling. She should have been in the back seat with some pimple-faced boy making out, or doing her homework.

I knew Rikki's father, Sylvester. We'd bonded through the embarrassing names we'd been saddled with. He was now known simply as Sy, and any reference to the original would lead to a war. At one time, Sy owned a blue BMW cycle with circus lights, a trailer, and those streamer things hanging from the hand grips. One of those dream toys, like Brooklyn Decker, or a Japanese massage, that life would go on very well without having but made one smile just thinking about it.

Giving up his motorcycle and the gang, Sy's time was spent collecting, and emptying, beer steins. His wife, I forgot her name, Giselle or something, left the day after Rikki was brought home from the hospital. The last he saw of her was walking out the door with a small suitcase, waving her arm and spouting, "I'm not ready for this shit."

The tiny pink package that came gift wrapped in a diaper became Sy's life, and he'd done a beautiful job in raising her.

My attention back on Rikki, sitting so still behind the wheel of a machine designed to overcome force and evil, I saw a little girl with a blonde ponytail. Looking so much like a child, she was a paradox. If I could have, I'd adopt her and send her off to a school so nothing would harm her, either herself or her mind.

She looked at me and I saw the vulnerability behind those large infectious gentle blue eyes, and the question she was waiting to ask but didn't know how to form the words. I made it easy, telling her, "Yeah, he was shot as punishment by some mean dudes. He did, or didn't, do something and it was wrong so he paid the price." Since I never wore a seatbelt, turning to her was easy. "Look, Rikki, guys like that have a choice to go to school and become teachers, or get a job in Wal-Mart, drive a forklift, or get connected to guns, killing and stealing. I don't feel anything for scum that make their living hurting people. At one time he was positioned to kill me, and he didn't think twice about doing it. He paid the price."

She was straining to keep from spilling tears, but one got out anyway. Wiping it away, she feigned a smile, "I haven't seen this side of the job before. I've been asking Lieutenant Grosslein to put me in the field but all I got were more reports to file." She paused, adding, "This doesn't change anything. I'm determined to be a good cop, Norby. I still want to get out and do some good in the community. Seeing a guy with a bullet in his head is not what I expected, but I'm looking at it as a beginning to be a cop."

"You already are a cop, honey. And a good one." I reached over to put my finger under a strand of errant blonde hair that had fallen over her eye, coaxing it back where it belonged. "Okay, I'm with you. Now that you got a taste of street cop stuff, stay on top of this. Follow the stiff to the ME's lab and get involved with the autopsy. Maybe Grossy will take a different look at his new Barbie-Cop."

Smiling, she cranked the engine to life and told me, "Screw you, Norby."

I'd like to, but that would be a violation I couldn't imagine happening. Before we got to the station, I asked, "You got a boyfriend?"

That infectious smile again, "Why? You lonesome?"

"No, I'm just trying to get to know who you are. A bright girl as cute as you would seem to have some kind of guy hanging around."

Looking into her lap, she revealed a secret crush. "Well, there is one guy. Brian. He works at Hell Burger."

Not totally surprised at her choice, "Melland? Brian Melland? The guy who's eating M&M's all the time?"

"You know him?"

"Yeah, he's a cool dude. He paid for my meal once when I was too drunk to get my hand in my pocket."

"Yeah, that's him. I think he's cute."

The smile was traded for a solemn glance, and her fantasy ended. "As soon as they find out I'm a cop, they all run away. And no, I refuse to date another cop." Then, to put a finish to my snooping, she added, "And, old washed-up private eyes that get cushy jobs as consultants."

Ouch. "I guess I'll have to take my lust elsewhere. You don't mind if I hang around as a watchdog, do you?"

Firm, she made her answer clear. "I don't need a watchdog, Norby."

"How about a friend?"

Pulling into the parking spot, the smile came back. "Friend is good. And very welcome. A friend with a zipper on his mouth and his pants that won't slide open, is a nice thing for a washed up rent-a-cop."

While Officer Thielges wrote out her report, I lounged in Grossy's office waiting to get invited for lunch. It never happened, but my little blonde friend broke the ice by dancing in with her report, typed in triplicate.

In a bubbly address, she handed Grossy another paper. Grumbling, he grated out, "What's this?"

Standing on her tip toes, she leaned over, explaining, "A request for computers in the squad room. Typing these reports on World War II typewriters is archaic. All you big shots have them and all you use them for is surfing pornography. Bring us into the twenty-first century, boss."

Grossy's eyebrows fell over his face, mumbling, "You hand me this crap once a week, Thielges. We don't have the money. My answer is always the same."

She handed him another paper, "The budget has set aside funds that are being used for personal items by management. Order computers before some silly clerk files this paper work in the wrong in-box and the mayor sees where the city's dedicated funds are going."

Pushing back in his wooden castered chair, he squeaked to a stop, "Are you blackmailing me, Thielges?"

Her answer, bright and perky, "Yes, sir, I am." She smiled sweetly.

Tossing the infected papers aside, he growled, "Fine. Now, where's the report on the shooting at Hell Burger?"

"Under your elbow. I just gave it to you."

Dumb as a mud fence, he lifted his saggy arm, "Oh. Well what about the shooting at the water plant?"

Exasperated, she leaned over his desk, "Here, under the one you just wrinkled leaning on." She took all the reports, shuffled them into shape, and handed them back. Sharply chastising the lieutenant, she chirped, "Which one of us is the boss here, boss? First things first. One, the Hell Burger shooting. Two, today's water plant shooting. And, three, don't forget the requisition for computers."

Defeated and overwhelmed, he scribbled his name on the requisition and handed it back. "Here, take the damn thing upstairs to the mayor's office yourself. Then get with that computer nerd and order what you need."

Dancing up and down, Rikki clapped her hands, "Yea, I'm getting a computer."

"Do it now, Thielges. I want to talk to our consultant, alone."

We both watched her skip out of the office, staring in appreciative wonderment.

In an unexpected show of human emotion, Stu smiled, "I'd be lost without her." Saving his masculinity, he turned to me, "Now, dipshit, what about the shooting at Hell Burger?"

"It's all in the report, Stu. The wrinkled one."

Gritting his teeth, he became hostile. "Tell me. What were you doing with her? She's been in and out of detox and treatment more than you have."

"The guy she was shacking up with got abusive, so she hid out at Hell Burger. I told her I'd get her drunk and take her home. That appealed to her, so after last call we went outside. I think she was going to kiss me when she disintegrated."

It all flashed back. I started to get the shakes again recalling the sound of the slug hitting and the sting of her pieces flying into my face.

Shit.

Stu showed a touch of compassion by just keeping his mouth shut. After a respectable amount of time, he said, "The guy she was living with, did you see any trace of him?"

"No. She told me he was screaming and breaking things in the apartment when she boogied. No sign of him at all."

"Clete Michaels. We've got an APB on him. He'll show up before too long."

"Stu, Clete might be an abusive ass hole, but he didn't shoot Angie."

"You don't know that, do you!"

"Yeah, Stu, I do know that." Now I started getting pissed. "Stu, Angie was no accident. Clete wasn't the shooter. She was killed as a sign to me that Kathleen Pierpont is back. I felt the second slug before it hit the wall. It was that close. I saw the car leave. It was in no hurry. Hanky thinks he saw a shadow creeping around my building. It was her."

In a fatherly tone, Stu said, "Bull shit. That recluse sees pink elephants. We're gonna find Clete Michaels and put this to bed."

Arguing was useless, and so was the help from the police. I was on my own here, and I was going to have to be a survivor. Just like on TV. Outwit, outplay, and outsmart the opponent. A ruthless psychotic murdering maniac. With a great ass.

CHAPTER
FIVE

● ● ● ● ● ● ● ● ● ● ● ● ● ● ● ● ● ● ● ●

OFFICER LORETTA THIELGES, CLUTCHING THE REQUEST form giving the city of Duluth orders to buy her a computer, bounced out of the precinct and headed upstairs to the mayor's office. Handing the form to the receptionist, she was told, "Sorry, honey, but we don't handle this. Take it to the accounting and procurement office." Taking the paper back, she was directed down the hall. Just as she reached the door, the mayor himself stepped to the receptionist with a file folder.

Glancing at the blonde pony-tailed policewoman, he asked his receptionist, "Who's that?" His voice was unusually quick with an obvious interest in the exiting cop.

"An officer with a budget request. I sent her . . ."

Just as the door closed, Rikki got her bearings and started for the proper office. Behind her, she heard, "Miss. Hey, there. Officer, wait."

She turned to the loud voice, and there he was, Don Ness, the mayor, in person. Rikki looked around, but she was the only one in the hallway, with the mayor quickly stepping to her. "Wait up."

"Me?" Unbelieving, she gawked at the rather handsome man sporting a natural invasion of gray to his well-groomed head. Panting, he said, "Yes, you." Inhaling to collect his system, "Whew, I'm really out of shape."

"Confused and starting to get frightened, she asked, "Me? You called for me?"

"Yes, I'd like to talk to you. Do you have a minute?"

Turning her head back to where she really wanted to go, she submitted, "Uhm, yes, of course. I guess so. Me?"

"Good, come with me. There's someone else I'd like you to meet."

Hesitating, Rikki's feet finally did their job and followed the mayor back to his office. Ushered through the waiting room, she exchanged shoulder shrugs with the receptionist. The mayor opened the door to his office and motioned her inside. One man she recognized as the police chief, and another unknown man stood as she stepped hesitantly into the chamber.

The mayor tossed a cryptic comment to the two men, "Look what I found. Our answer, right?" The beaming smile at his discovery had Rikki feeling like a prize at a slave auction.

The mayor hustled past her, "You must know the chief of police, Gordon Ramsay, from the Arlington office, and this is Frank Tellworth, Duluth FBI agent."

Chief Ramsay stepped forward offering his hand, and at his touch, Rikki felt the red crawl over her face. The strong presence and obvious magnetism of the ambrosial man had an electrifying effect on her. Timid and insecure, she blubbered, "Yes, sir. Chief Ramsay, glad to meet you," although she had no idea why. Her eyes floated on the clean-shaven youthful face of the chief and the redness in her face shot down her body to her knees, which were failing to support her.

The chief glanced at her name tag, "Officer Thielges. I've seen you in the precinct, but I don't think we've ever met. Sorry about that."

Stumbling with a response, she could only muster, "Oh, yeah." And offered a shaky smile. She could only imagine she had a piece of something stuck to her teeth, or typewriter ink spread over her face. Damn.

The other man, short and quite thin, with an artificial neatness about him, stepped into her gawking of the chief. "Officer. I'm Frank Tellworth, Duluth FBI. How are you?"

Returning the pumping of his firm grip, she sputtered, "Huh? How am I? I don't know."

The mayor seated himself behind the large walnut desk, "Officer Thielges, please sit down, and for heavens sake relax. We aren't going to bite you." She strained from glancing at the chief, thinking that's exactly what she wanted him to do.

Still clutching her papers, she lowered herself into a leather upholstered chair, leaning forward. Her hands and legs had become obstructions she didn't know what to do with. To load up her insecurity, an imbecilic grin did nothing to help with her composure. The mayor opened with, "Officer Thielges, we were just in a discussion that had reached a dead end because we had a problem we didn't know how to deal with. When, by chance, I saw you in the office, it became clear, to me anyway, that you might be able to help us."

Those large blue eyes darted from one man to the next, and all she could think of was, "Huh?"

He looked to the other men for support, and Chief Ramsay asked, "You work in the squad room, right?"

In a pubescent croak, she muttered, "Yes, sir. I mainly type reports and make coffee." Her face lit up and she brightly added, "But today, Norby Klein and I went to a crime scene and I processed it. There was a dead man at the water plant." Out of breath, she sat back, waiting for this scene to make sense.

Frank Tellworth spoke up, "Officer Thielges, how long have you been on the force?"

Her answer was quick and sure, "Three years, sir."

The big question for her was, FBI?

The mayor interjected, "We'll pull your file and get the details. Officer Thielges, we need help in a case, and I just think you'd work out very well. Would you consider a special assignment?" He leaned over, waiting.

She looked from one man to the next, totally unnerved by the sudden attention. Her mind racing, she calculated that this was her chance. "I've been pounding out reports for three years, and learned how to make good cop coffee. Just today I told Norby Klein how much I wanted to prove myself to be a good officer. I want to do whatever it takes to be a good cop, but I have no idea what you're talking about. Shouldn't Lieutenant Grosslein know?"

Tellworth leaned forward, "Norby Klein?"

The mayor spoke. "He's a paid consultant. A private eye, really, but we keep him close. The Pierpont case, you know."

With a knowing nod, Tellworth said, "Oh, yeah. Do you think he'd be useful here?"

With a sigh, the mayor admitted, "Yes, I suppose so," but the enthusiasm had left him. Turning to Officer Thielges, "We'll get Stu Grosslein involved when the time is right. In the meantime, I'll notify him that you are being pulled into a special task force we're forming."

Rikki's response, "Oh, wow. What do I do now?"

"Why don't you just go back to work until we can work out the details. Don't mention this to anybody, even Lieutenant Grosslein. Understand?"

"Yeah, sure. I guess so."

The FBI suddenly asked, "Officer Thielges, are you married? Do you have children?"

Now she got concerned and wondered if he was going to ask her for a date, or was this still business. Capped with a frown, she answered, "No, I'm not married and have no children. I live alone. What do . . . ?"

The mayor stood to prevent an awkward situation, "We'll look in your file to get what we need on a personal level. Don't worry. By the way, where were you headed before I kidnapped you?"

Taken back by the change in the topic, she stammered, "Uh, to the accounting office. I'm submitting a request for a computer."

Reaching out, he asked, "Is that the request? Let me see it."

Passing it over to him, she stood, unsure of what was going to happen.

"Hmm, looks good, but with a computer you'll need a printer and IT back-up. I'll see that this gets taken care of." He looked up with a genuine campaign-style smile designed to win her vote. "Go back to work and we'll notify you. It should be soon."

Everyone shook hands and exchanged smiles, Rikki finally understanding her time here was up. Passing the receptionist, she gave her a "beats me" grin.

Watching her close the door to his office, the mayor queried the other two, "What do you think? She looks good for the part. My opinion is that she'd be ideal with a shape like that, and a perfect blonde? If she'll do it."

They all nodded agreement. Chief Ramsay, added, "I'll pull her file and see if there are any hang-ups. If she's clean and can get through what we explain about the job, she'd be perfect."

The mayor closed the meeting with, "Come back tomorrow at nine. Gordy, if you think she's a good pick we'll get her back up here."

Gordon Ramsay went to the personnel office, asking to be left in privacy. Thumbing through the files, he came to, Thielges, Loretta A. He stepped over to the drawer labeled, K, and pulled, Klein, Norbert. No middle initial. After inquiring about the report she filed on the water plant shooting, he locked himself in his office to do his homework. He was determined to make the right choice here, worried that if this assignment wasn't handled with the utmost care and planning, Officer Thielges life would positively be in danger.

CHAPTER
SIX

● ●

I REASONED IT WOULD BE A BLESSING TO SOCIETY if Clete Michaels was in jail. But, as much as I loathed the bastard, I would object to his being charged with shooting Angie. Her death was just days ago and I hadn't been able to sleep since. Lying in the dark, listening to the mice battle with the cockroaches, I couldn't get away from the sight of her face, blown to pieces. When things did quiet down, and the liquor had stupefied my brain into oblivion, I was jolted back to the real world and recalled the splat of the bullet hitting her face. After that I wouldn't dare risking sleep and the nightmares it would hold.

If Kathleen Pierpont was not the one holding the rifle, she was close by prodding to get it done. The favors she had to offer as a reward to her madness were considerable, and I was sure she chose her eunuch carefully. She was not the first person who wanted me dead, or tried to make me dead, but certainly the most frightening.

So, now what? I needed to do something to stay alive, and to make that happen I needed to find Kathleen Pierpont. I could assume she knew where I was at all times so she had the advantage. As long as I was visible, she was going to make a move, taunting and teasing.

Outwit, outplay, outsmart.

I had to get the upper hand, forcing her in the open to come after me, instead of lurking at her convenience. I did know a few things about her that would help with the profile. Her father got her pregnant at age eleven, then forced her into an abortion in Sweden. Her hatred for men was understandable. She needed medication to sleep, to stay awake, to maintain a normal nervous system, to stem serious depression, to calm her alpestrine sexual rages, and after all that, I imagined there was one to keep her from twitching.

If she had operating capital, that would complicate things. Whatever her resources, she'd use whatever it took to avenge my screwing up her operation.

I couldn't see her using a disguise as an effective cover-up. At five-foot-nine, with the body of a goddess and a face beyond belief, there was no place to hide. She'd had help escaping the police when her mother shot her as she was in the act of beheading me, so I assumed she had a toad in tow to do the dirty work.

All right, with that said, I wasn't without resources myself. I thought. My next move would be to contact my partners at Pink Power Investigations. If I was being watched, I didn't want to announce my involvement with the pink investigators. I flipped open my cell phone and called the office.

"Pink Power Investigations, may I help you?"

Ahh, the sweet melodic tones of my ever faithful Jeanine. I knew she'd be happy to hear me, "Hi, honey, how are you."

"Oh, Norby, what do you want?"

"Don't sound so glum. I just wanted to talk to my business partners. You busy?"

"For you, yes, we're busy." She covered the mouthpiece on the phone and called out to Brew, "It's Klein. You want to talk to him?" After the muffled response, she came back. "Yeah, we're busy."

It was obvious she loved me.

Now I had to get serious. "Jeanine, I really need your help."

"Hire a hooker. Just don't get her shot like the last one. Angie, right?"

"Yeah, Jeanine, Angie." I let a moment pass and told her, "Kathleen Pierpont is back. She's the one who shot Angie. She's trying to spook me."

I felt her coming back to earth, on my side. Her voice more somber, "What do you need, Norbs?"

"I want to get together with you and Brew to see how we can smoke her out. It can't be at the office, though. I think I'm being watched."

"Wait a minute." Talking to the muffled voice again, she came back, "Keep your cell on. I'll get back to you." As a parting thought, she told me, "Stay out of sight, Norby."

"Thanks." Now what do I do? Pondering this, my cell phone chirped. Thinking that Jeanine was on the other end, I said, "Hi, honey."

"Don't get mushy, you dope." It was Stu Grosslein.

"Uh, oh. I thought it ..."

"Then stop thinking before you hurt yourself. At nine tomorrow morning we have a meeting with the mayor and the chief. Be here on time and for God's sake, be sober."

"What the hell do I have to do with the mayor? Am I in trouble?"

"I'd be surprised if you weren't in trouble, Klein. Nine tomorrow. Be on time."

Grossy hung-up before I could discover that he didn't know anymore about this than I did. The mayor speaketh, and we jumpeth.

Jeanine never called back, not because she didn't love me anymore. I was certain Brew ate all the telephones. The mayor obviously had me in his cross-hairs, so the pink investigators would be put on hold. I was sure they wouldn't mind.

The meeting with his eminence, the lord holy Don Ness, was at nine. At nine-thirty, I sauntered into Stu's office begging for coffee and forgiveness. Detective Lieutenant Stuart Grosslein had burst a safety valve with steam shooting from his hairy nostrils. I greeted him, "Hey, Grossy, what's shakin'?"

His voice was a spit-infested hiss that told me I was a some kind of something and he hated me. No coffee I guessed. "You, you, you piece of . . . I told you nine."

I put my hand on his shoulder to keep him from leaping on me. I followed this with sound reasoning. "Grossy, if you don't stop erupting, we're gonna be late."

He walked ahead of me, which was fine. A rear assault would just not be good. Outside the mayor's office, he harrumphed a couple times, straightened his tie, which was tied too tight, emphasizing his neck fat. In a harsh whisper, he warned me, "Let me do the talking. You're out of your element here. Let's go in."

While Stu was charming the receptionist to gain our audience with the mayor, I stepped over to the visitors' chairs and asked, "Rikki, what are you doing here?"

She was sitting straight up, beaming that infectious smile at me. I wanted to kiss her head and put her on a school bus. "Chief Ramsay called me last night at home. I was told to be here this morning. What are you doing here?"

"I think he wants to give me an award. What's going on?"

She leaned forward, cupping her hand to her mouth, "I was here yesterday and . . . I can't tell you any more. Something's up. I'm supposed to wait here."

At that point, Stu grabbed me and did a double-step when he spotted his clerk typist. "Thielges?" More steam.

Saving the imminent comedic routine of "who's on first" or "what are you doing here," the mayor's door opened with the great man waving us in. Rikki dutifully stayed where she was, swinging her feet under the chair.

I've been in the mayor's office before when he asked me to do counter-intelligence work on an officer suspected of beating his wife. Don Ness and I had become close when we worked together getting counseling help for the officer, and a safe house for his wife. I went the extra mile and went with the cop to his sessions, then became a crying post for a man who was truly sorry and ashamed of what he did. They were back together and the beatings had stopped. The work on their relationship was going through some rough terrain.

To Grossy's annoyance Don and I clasped hands as if we were in a lodge club meeting. Secret hand shakes and all. Chief of Police Gordy Ramsay and a guy I recognized as a fed stood up to exchange secret hand shakes. The mayor's authoritive voice said, "Gentlemen, shall we get started?"

On cue we all sat down, familiar with each other, except for the fed, and why he was here. Grossy and I didn't know why we were here either. "Mr. Tellworth, would you like to start?" It was not a question, but did get things rolling.

The small statured fed stood up, resplendent in his black suit. I wouldn't be a bit surprised if Will Smith and Tommy Lee Jones were sitting with us. "Okay, gentlemen, we have a problem, and the five of us are going to make it go away. Well, us and one other person."

My mind immediately ran into the outer office where Rikki was waiting. Oh, shit.

He continued, "The Duluth FBI office has been working their way into a ring of smugglers who have moved into the Duluth harbor. It's been a problem tying down what they've been doing because we think it isn't what they're bringing in to the port, but what they are taking out. And, we have no idea what it is."

Of course, my being a smart ass, I piped up, "Then how do you know there's even a problem?"

"Good question, Mr. Klein. We had a couple agents infiltrate the ship's crew. One agent disappeared and turned up in the port of Antalya, in Turkey. Stashed in the hull of a ship, mutilated. The same ship he was instrumental in helping to load, right here in Duluth. The other agent was pulled and sent to another assignment." He looked at Chief Ramsay, "Chief, the rest is from your end, so you can take it from here."

The chief stood, and I realized why I respected the man so much. He was the boss.

"Okay, where to begin. Um, it's obvious with the resources we have that sending agents into the crew is too dangerous." He cast a sympathetic glance at Mr. Tellworth. "While we know who the crew members are, and where they live and hang out, we don't know the king-pins. Who runs the show. While ashore, they don't cause too many problems, and at the time, the citizens are safe. Our plan is, instead of infiltrating, we observe. Their hangout is mainly the Conestoga Club. Naturally, the strippers are a draw. They've been spotted in Hell Burger, but Mitch Omer say's they are all right. We are going to plant one of our officers as a waitress in the Conestoga…"

At the mention of that, the top of my head blew off, and I voiced my objection, "Gordy, you can't mean Officer Thielges."

While Stu recoiled with embarrassment at my outburst, the mayor stood over his desk, "Klein, calm down and hear him out." He held his hands out as a gesture to keep peace and good will among us. Shit.

"Yes, Norby, I mean Officer Thielges. I've talked to her, looked over her file, and checked as much as I could. She'd be perfect for the job. Of course, the final decision is up to her. If she wants out, she's out with no regrets or recrimination of any kind." Yeah, and we all knew that would be an albatross in her file.

Gordy looked at me, "Klein, the reason you're here is to be her back-up. You are a familiar character in the place so you won't be noticed. Officer Thielges is an unknown. Now, I'd like to get her in here and see if she's willing to take it on."

As he stepped to the door, I stood in front of him. "Wait. I want someone else on hand."

I got a quizzical look from everyone except Stuart Grosslein. He was busy catching his breath and returning his face color back to pink. "I want my own plant at the bar. I know a woman who'd be perfect. Who better than a six-foot-three woman with a great ass and set of hoo-hoos to watch over a room full of murdering dock hands?"

The mayor, the fed, and the chief, looked at each other, until Gordy asked, "Can we get funds to pay her?"

Mayor Ness nodded, and asked me, "Can we get her in to talk to her?"

"I'll work it out. When does this all take place?"

Tellworth answered, "This is Wednesday, we'd like to get it going for the Friday crowd. We'll put a bug on the officer, and after we see if your hoo-hoo-enriched woman is going to work, we'll bug her as well."

The mayor nodded to the chief, who then opened the door. "Officer Thielges, would you come in please?"

CHAPTER
SEVEN

● ● ● ● ● ● ● ● ● ● ● ● ● ● ● ● ● ● ●

RIKKI CAUTIOUSLY STEPPED INTO THE CARPETED sanctuary with the look of a new girl in a strange class on the first day of school. I could tell she was too frightened to smile. Looking over the crowd of male eyes staring her, she brought her hand up, waved it once and meekly said, "Hi."

I stood and offered her my chair, as the mayor prompted, "Officer Thielges, please, have a seat."

As she lowered her butt into the chair, she looked at me. All I saw was fear and doubt in her eyes. I put my hand on her shoulder to ease her back into safety.

The mayor came from behind the sanctity of his over-sized desk to sit on the front edge. Just like a regular joe. Through his smile, intentionally softened for effect, he softly spoke, "Loretta, how are you?"

Her response was truthful, as only Rikki could give it. "Scared shitless. How are you?"

His smile broadened. "When you were in here talking to us earlier, we said there was a special operation we thought you'd be perfect for. We'll let Chief Ramsay outline it for you, and if you don't like it, there's nothing more to say. It will be your choice with no pressure. Okay?"

She nodded her head to the side, "I guess so."

The chief sat back, trying to look relaxed. "May I call you Loretta?"

A nod again. "Yeah, whatever." Her responses all had question marks attached.

Going over the details of the dock crew and loading ships, even the details about the slain agent, he got into the meat and potatoes of this whole thing. "We want you to pose as a waitress at the Conestoga Club, wearing a wire, hanging around the dock crew, picking up comments and talk about what they're doing. Norbert has a woman who may pose as a bartender to back you up."

I cringed at the use of my full name.

"A satellite van will be outside recording everything you hear. At any time you feel threatened, or compromised, we want you to get out and go to the back room. Agent Tellworth will have agents back there to help you. And, of course, Mr. Klein will be in the audience watching you all the time."

I nodded appreciation for using a more appropriate name for me.

I kneaded her shoulder and she put her hand on mine, squeezing. She was scared to death. I told her, "It's up to you, Rikki. Say no and there won't be any questions. Think about it."

She looked at me with that prom queen smile, and I knew this was going to be a big mistake. Scanning the others, she had made up her mind. "Yeah, sure. As long as I know there's someone watching, and I have a way out, I'll do it."

Smiles came from everyone but me. I clinched her shoulder tighter, and now I was scared to death. She asked, "What do I do now?"

The fed stood up, "Go home and put on some civvies, and meet me at my office." He handed her his too-expensive embossed card bearing the address of the Duluth FBI office.

A branch of the Minneapolis office, the Duluth FBI was relatively small in comparison to the others across the nation. However, the range of responsibility ran from Minnesota to North and South Dakota. Located in the Federal Building on West First Street, Rikki had no doubt where to go.

The meeting was over, but a few more loose ends were covered by rambling details and suggestions tossed about. I took special interest in Detective Lieutenant Grosslein's silence through the whole proceeding. He huffed out, brushing past me without one disparaging comment. That was unusual.

I waited outside the open door, until Rikki was done nodding her head to indicate she understood. We walked together out to the parking lot and I stood with her beside the dark blue 1968 GT 390 Mustang she drove. Every time I looked at her car the entire movie, *Bullitt*, with Steve McQueen racing over the San Francisco streets banged through my mind. I asked her, once more, "You sure you won't trade this for my Reliant?"

Her laugh was just as hypnotizing as her smile. "Someday, Norbs. Not yet."

She knew I was going to get serious, so I cut through the banter, "Are you certain about this, honey?"

"This is what I've wanted for so long. Yes, I'm positive."

"Want me to go with you to the Federal Building?"

"No, but I'm gonna want you with me when this starts. I'll talk to you in the office tomorrow and let you know what's happening."

I stood back while the Mustang rumbled, the prom queen goosing all 390 cubic inches into a 335-horse-power frenzy. As she laid rubber, she called back, "I get my computer tomorrow."

Watching her drive away, I wanted to cry.

Making sure Rikki got out of the parking lot without being abducted by space aliens, and went home to put her mind in the right place, I had three stops to make. The first was at the Conestoga Club to see my friend Louie, the manager. Built like Sasquatch, but twice as hairy, Louie's presence alone was frightening, until he talked, and walked. I taught him to quit waving his hand like he was tossing flowers at a gay rights parade, which he'd done, and to simply let his hairy bulk do the intimidating for him.

He caught sight of me entering through the back door, and his face lit up. I hoped he wasn't going to hug me.

"Norbert Klein, how good of you to drop in."

That name boo-boo again.

Keeping enough distance between us, I asked, "Louie, you're aware of what's going on?"

"I know enough to stay safe, Norbs. How about you?"

I didn't want to play a fencing game with him. It was made clear in the meeting that Louie was aware and cooperating. I needed to test the water before saying something stupid. "Anything I should know about?"

He sat on a bar stool and stared at me. I wanted to strangle him, but my hands weren't big enough. I waded into the water a little deeper. "I was at a meeting with the mayor and a couple of other guys."

He just sat there, doing his own water testing.

"I'm going to be a part of it." I dangled a little bait, and he reasoned it was safe to talk. I wanted to hug him for being discrete, but got over it.

He glanced around to assure we were alone. "Yeah, I'm aware of what's happening." This is the first time I'd ever seen him so serious.

I opened with, "An undercover cop's going to waitress in here. She'll be wearing a bug, and I have someone I want to plant as a bartender."

"That's fine, but they better be lookers or the place will get trashed."

"Believe me, Louie, they're both lookers. I'll be hanging around in here as my usual drunken self as back-up. I want to know if it's going to be safe."

"Yeah, Norbs. I don't see no problem. The guys you're talking about don't make too much noise, or fuss any more than the usual stiff in here. However, if you plan on screwing with 'em, better send Godzilla to do it."

The chill of reality hit my face like an ice storm off the lake. My frown spoke for me, prompting Louie's response. "Mean. They're mean mothers, man. Big guys. Quiet, but they got a mean look."

"So, besides watching the strippers, what their purpose here?"

He threw his paws into the air showing his disgust at my ignorance. "Watching strippers. What else do guys come in here for?"

"This cop, Louie, the waitress. She'll be hanging around these guys trying to pick up some talk about what they might be doing outside. She'll bring the drinks and fuss with the table, eavesdropping. The bartender I plant will keep a close eye on her. I understand there'll be some agents in the back room in case something happens."

"I ain't worried." The smile on Louie's face reminded me of King Kong when he fell in love with Fay Wray. "Do I have to pay these women, Norbs?"

"No, we'll let the taxpayers do that." I had something else to tell my hairy friend, and it made me nervous. "Louie, this cop; the waitress—she's special and I want her safe."

Waving his massive arms, instead of swinging from trees, he walked away chortling, "What's not safe? Serve booze and laugh at demeaning sexist cheap remarks from a room full of drunks watching naked strippers. Geez."

My second stop would have a little more understanding. I stepped through the door of the Pink Power Investigations office and waited while a sobbing woman was escorted out. Jeanine, with an arm over the woman's shoulder, holding a check in her hand, softened whatever made her blubber so. "Don't worry, honey. We're gonna fry his ass good. Just don't say anything to anyone." We watched as the sobbing lady drove away in a black Mercedes, Jeanine waving the check in triumph. "One more ass-hole down the drain." She and Brew high-fived and admired the string of numbers on the check.

Brew finally decided I was worthy of attention. "What the hell do you want?"

Offering my nicest defensive smile, "You always make me feel so welcome in my own office. Jeanine, Brew, you both look ravishing today."

Brew's comment was less painful than a hammer lock, "Fuck you, ass-hole."

Jeanine, the faithful companion, stepped in, "Hear him out, honey." Giving me a fierce glance, she asked, "What were you getting at on the phone?"

"Oh, yeah, the phone. I'm still waiting for you to call back. Come on, girls, I work here too. You know, all men are not jerks."

Jeanine's logic had me stumped, "Yeah, and some day we'll meet one."

"Cut me some slack. I come bearing gifts of glad tidings and good will. I have a job for both of you."

Brew was quick with, "If the blow word is attached to it, your gonna hang up-side down in a meat locker."

I put on my serious look, "No, not that. A real job of surveillance. The Duluth PD and the feds have a sting in play and needs a rook." I beamed a smile and applied my charm. "Brew, you would be a perfect fit for it. I've already got approval to get you involved."

Jeanine, always suspicious, especially of me, asked, "What is it?"

"At the Conestoga Club, Friday night. You in?" I was hopeful.

She repeated the earlier comment, "Fuck you, ass-hole."

Brew stepped in, "What's it pay?"

Grabbing desperately at straws, I tried using logic. "When it comes to public service, the price is incidental. What about the good of the public and all that?"

Amazonia stood up, towering over me, and grabbed my shirt front. "Listen, dirt-wad, how much?"

Choking, I rasped out, "I think you can bill them for at least a couple of grand. That'd be nice, wouldn't it?"

She released her vice-grip on my shirt. "What do we do?"

Brew planted her million dollar ass on the edge of her desk. "Tell us what's going on, and tell us all of it. If there's any snags I'm not aware of, don't forget that meat locker I mentioned."

Now that she had instilled me with confidence, I explained the gig, making certain they knew it was dangerous. "There's a mob working as dock workers who are shipping out something, but nobody knows what it is. The feds are sure its illegal, and they had one of their agents planted, but he was killed.

"The bulk of the goons involved are mainly acting as dock hands and have taken to using the Conestoga as a way to let off steam. A gathering place. They spend the night looking at strippers and making obnoxious lewd comments. Sometimes they request some special treatment from the stage ladies, but nobody knows where that takes place."

Now, I was dead serious, and I could tell they believed my sincerity. "Brew, I want you to get in as a bartender to keep an eye on the cop posing as a waitress. Get to know her and keep the dialog going between you. The cop'll have a bug with a van outside to pick it all up. There'll be feds in the back in case there's a glitch. Jeanine, I want you to sit with me and act like a drunk's girlfriend."

Her logic was overwhelming. "Not like I haven't done that before."

I expected an outburst with Brew, whipping out the meat hook. Instead, Jeanine and Brew looked at each other and I knew a message went between them. The simple nod was an understanding. They were both in. When Jeanine stepped to the front door and locked it, my knees got weak, and I pictured the inside of a meat locker, hanging by my heels. Brew shut off the office lights and motioned me into the conference room that used to be my office. The only illumination was from a small fluorescent lamp on the walnut conference table. Jeanine closed the office door and I was alone with them. Perfect, no witnesses.

Instead of turning me upside down and piercing my tendons with a meat hook, I was invited to sit down. Maybe they were just going to beat me to death. Much better than dying in a freezer.

They seated themselves on either side of me, Jeanine speaking quietly. "Norby, that woman you saw when you got here is Gloria Fields. Her husband, Burton, owns the Great Lakes Shipping Company. She hired us to find out what he's doing in his spare time. Strangers have been showing up at their home, and the description she gives has them in a different social setting than she's used to. She called them rough and crude, with foreign accents. They bring women into the house, and she's frightened to death about what they are doing. Liquor, noise, the women getting naked."

While that sounded like my kind of party, I could imagine the fear that Mrs. Fields must feel. "Has she mentioned why its taking place in her home? And, all of a sudden?"

Brew stepped in, becoming involved in the conversation. I was totally taken back by the sincere tone to her voice, and my life wasn't threatened at all. "Mr. Fields had been having money trouble. Her husband told her it was the economy affecting the shipping business. Then, after a visit from some unseemly types, the money problems seemed to get less. She's assuming he sold them all, or part, of the business. Since then he's been gone for days at a stretch and is acting erratic when he is home. She described him as more frightened than anything. He's remote with her and won't let her in. She confided with us that she thinks he's keeping her as far away from the problem as possible. A plus for him, but terrifying for her."

Jeanine leaned forward, "She asked us to see what we could find out. Her life has changed, and she's scared stiff." After a pause, she added, "We'll help with the Conestoga deal, but you have to stay with us to find out what's happening with Great Lakes Shipping."

"Yes, I'm in. Brew, show up at the club about six o'clock and ask for Louie. Tell him I sent you. Wear something provocative." My mind spun on that thought. "Jeanine, I'm taking Rikki in at six to get ready. Wait for me in the parking lot so we can go in together."

I looked from one to the other, hoping for a nod of approval. All I got was two sets of eyes glaring at me. Jeanine broke the spell, "Geez, Norbs, what else do you want? We'll be there."

As I was half out the door, Jeanine stopped me. "Norby, you mentioned Rikki. Is that the little blonde gal that works in the office?"

I started getting that chill again. "Yeah, she's the waitress."

"Are you sure? Hell, I'd do it instead of her."

"I wish it could be that way. You have no idea how worried I am. If she were to be taken out of the line-up now, she'd never be the same again. This is a big step for her to prove to herself that she can make it as a cop and be respected like the others. No, I don't like it, but there's no going back now."

She nodded, understanding.

The next stop was going to be difficult, but I owed the man the truth. Stopping in front of the house, I wished this was not happening. Located in an aging neighborhood up on the hill overlooking Duluth, the simple bungalow needed a paint job, a new roof, the cement steps were crumbling, and Christmas lights from 1988 were still hung with care. That was the year his wife left with no intention of returning, leaving Sy with a two-day old baby to care for. Sy had the money to make all the repairs. He was just poor in desire to get it done.

My tapping on the tattered screen door got an answer after a few moments. "Hi, Sy. Got a minute to talk?" He stood aside to let me in, and we man-hugged.

Sylvester Thielges was a big man. In many ways. First, his heart was the big kind that always had time to listen to your problem, or loan you a buck or two, or to just be a friend. The other big part of him was his bulk. A retired brick layer, he had built a physical stature that was impressive, if he wasn't mad at you. Sporting a billy goat beard, and an infectious laugh, he was a great guy. And, very protective of the love of his life, his daughter, Loretta.

One trait that Sy had that I found endearing, was when in any discussion he had an add-on for, he'd stick his thumb up and apply his wisdom, "The way I see's it is …"

And, he had no idea he was doing it.

I didn't quite know how to approach him on the subject of Rikki doing undercover work, but she had crossed that bridge for me. "Yeah, Rikki was here and told me all about her gig as a cop spy. I'm not sure I like it, but she was so excited, I had to go with it."

He handed me a Grain Belt Nordeast and asked, "Tell me, Norbs, is she gonna be all right? Is it safe?" The worry on his gnarled face tore through me. I had to be honest. He was my friend and I respected him enough to do that.

"That's why I'm here, Sy. I want you to know she'll have as much cover as possible. I'll be there with Jeanine, and our partner will be behind the bar. There'll be a knot of agents in the back, and a van outside will pick up conversation."

He pulled a long drag of beer, asking, "Do you think I should be there? To help?"

Bad idea and I had to squelch it. "No, Sy. Not even. If she knew her old man was in the audience, she'd get too nervous. Promise me you'll stay home."

He sunk into himself, feeling utterly useless. Looking up, his eyes said it all. He was scared to death. "Yeah, I know. I'll stay away."

"When it's over, I'll come by and tell you about it."

As quietly as I've ever heard him speak, "She really wants this, Norbs. She thinks its her step into the major leagues."

I knew the man was crying, but it was all inside. Hoarse and quiet, he rasped, "Yeah, I'll be waiting. And I wouldn't want to watch her anyway. I couldn't."

"She's a big girl, Sy. She wants to do this more than anything."

He took in a deep breath, "Yeah, I know."

I had to get out of there. I was crying also.

CHAPTER EIGHT

• •

I SHOULD HAVE GONE HOME RIGHT AWAY, but I needed to lubricate some things squeaking deep inside. Windsor and Pepsi worked just fine for stuff like that and Pappy automatically put it together as soon as I walked in. I took my office annex seat at the end of Hell Burgers bar, thanked him, and checked the little yellow note things stuck to the wall. There were seven of them, six of which suggested I have sex with myself. Predictably, I knew I probably would have to. The seventh note simply said someone hated me.

The true love of my life ambled up to me, "Hey, Norby, good to see you." Cynthia Gerdes always took time to make me feel at home, and made me keep my bar tab up to date. This time she had a concerned look.

"Hi, Cyn, as usual, you're gorgeous beyond belief. When are you going to dump Mitch and run away with me?"

She signaled Pappy, behind the bar, and took her diet Coke from him. "If I could be sure I wouldn't get shot, I'd take you up on that." She hoisted up to the stool, "How you doing? Any news on Angie's shooter? Did they find Clete?"

"They'll find him in time, but he's not the trigger."

"You seem certain about that."

"Yup. He's a hitter, and someday he probably would have killed Angie with his fists anyway, but he didn't do this."

Her head nodded slightly and she knew I was right. "Now what?"

I held my breath a moment, and then said, "Can't tell you."

She passed the half full diet across the bar and slid to the floor. She stuck her finger at my face as a loving gesture, "You take care, you hear?"

It was late when I stepped out of Hell Burger. I forgot where I left the car and settled on walking, unless someone offered to carry me. Angie's blood was permanently embedded in the asphalt outside. The woman was dead and all that

42

was left was a splotch of stuff that had at one time coursed through her veins. I suppose taking a bullet to the face was less painful than being beaten to death by a sociopathic bastard trying to hide behind his control of another human. No, Clete didn't shoot her, and at first I recoiled at his being hunted for it, but it might not be a bad idea to gun him down in a battle with the cops.

Shit.

It was late Wednesday, and show time was Friday. If I went home there was no chance of sleeping, so I did what I needed to do. After straining my sloshed mind to start working, I recalled where I left my classic Reliant. I stood in front of Hell Burger and saw it sitting just ten feet away. Duh.

I had no business bothering Rikki at, what time was it? Three in the morning? That couldn't be. Man, I had to get my shit together. Anyway, I sat in front of her apartment wondering if I had a right to invade her privacy. A light was glowing at one of her windows on the second floor, but that didn't necessarily mean she was awake.

I couldn't bring myself to barge in, so I turned the ignition key. While the Reliant was deciding on whether or not to start, I was jolted into next week by a voice. "Norby, what are you doing here?" I had never heard Rikki sound so fierce. Maybe she was practicing to be mean.

Clutching my chest, I gasped, "Holy shit."

"Are you spying on me?"

Through the intake of the oxygen my lungs were demanding, I managed, "Rikki, for chrissake, don't ever do that." The thought of a few days in the hospital cardiology ward had an appeal of resting quietly, and nurses giving rub downs. As usual, the timing was all wrong. "Spying, no. I was worried about you and drove over. I was about to leave when you attacked me." I had tunnel vision and my heart was pounding nails into my chest, but otherwise, hunky-dorrie.

"I told you, Norbert Klein, I do not need a baby sitter." I had a teacher that would speak to me in the same harsh voice. Ouch.

"Calm down and get in the damn car before a cop shows up."

She steamed around the front and slammed herself into the passenger seat. She folded her arms and lowered her forehead over her eyes, pouting. Her voice, quiet and sullen, "I am a cop."

My respiration was getting back to a normal beat, allowing me to actually talk like a grown up. "Rikki, calm down. You're so hell-bent on proving yourself as a cop, you're losing sight of why you are draining the swamp in the first place."

She wrinkled her nose and said, "Huh?"

"Never mind, just some old man logic. Nobody doubts that you're a cop. The chief's confidence in you proves that. I know I'm overprotective and can hover at times, but I'm allowed to do that. Enjoy the fact that I care about you like I would my own daughter. Yes, I'm worried about Friday, and so are you or you'd be asleep now."

She was clad in a tee shirt and tiny shorts, with low-cut tennies attached to her feet. Subdued now, "Yeah, I know. I know and I appreciate it. I think I have to prove myself to be respected, and I'm going to do it. You're right. I couldn't sleep so I went for a jog. I'll admit I'm worried, but that's a good thing."

"You know of course that you are plumb loco for being out here, in this neighborhood, scantily clad, in the dark."

Protesting, "I am not scantily clad. And," she brought her right foot up to the seat in a double joint move that amazed me, showing off the small leather holster strapped to her ankle that I had totally missed. "I'm packin', dude."

I was embarrassed, but felt very good now. "Okay, Bonnie Parker, you made your point."

That look again. "Huh? Bonnie who?"

"Bonnie and Clyde. Forget it. So, what went on at the FBI office?"

"They showed me the bug and how to use it, and a few things to watch for."

I added what I had. "I'll have my partner, Brewskie the Horrible, tending bar and I'll be there with Jeanine as back up. Take a moment to work out a signal system with Brew, and get her involved with what you see and do. She's a resourceful ally. What are you doing tomorrow?"

"I'm going fishing with my dad. Why don't you come with?"

"I'd love to, honey, but that's time for you and your dad only. Convince him you know what you're doing and you'll be safe. He's a basket case of worry, and doesn't know how to handle it."

"I can handle him. You should have seen him on my prom night. Like an old lady. It's hereditary with the Thielges. They all just worry."

She turned to me with that sweet look again and my heart melted, telling me, "If I didn't have my dad as dad, I'd want you. Thanks. I feel better now." Up on her knees, she leaned over and planted a peck on my cheek. She rubbed my face and said, "You need a shave."

I watched her bound up the steps and waited until the light in her window went out. She was such a sweetheart. And, I was scared shitless for what she was about to do.

CHAPTER NINE

● ● ● ● ● ● ● ● ● ● ● ● ● ● ● ● ● ● ● ●

Friday afternoon I picked up Rikki at her apartment. She was clad in faded jeans with the left knee worn through, and a maroon UMD sweatshirt that was long enough for her finger tips to barely peek out the sleeve holes. Dragging a small backpack, she climbed into the Reliant and set it between her feet. Thrusting her finger to the windshield, emulating John Wayne leading the cavalry, she bellowed, "Yoooohhh."

That wasn't enough to get me moving. I looked at her. "Should we circle the wagons?"

I should have expected her smart-ass comment, "If that's what it takes for you to wake up and punch the pedal, yeah, circle away."

So I did. If it were possible, I'd impress her by laying a strip of front wheel rubber, but the most the Plymouth would give me was a cloud of smoke. The first stop was at my former but now shared office, to pick up Jeanine. Inside, Jeanine and Rikki gave each other a gal hug, while Brew just offered a handshake. Appreciative that Brew didn't pull a kung-foo move and toss Rikki over her shoulder, I thought they might just get along with each other.

Jeanine, my date for tonight, was clad in jeans that were painted on, low healed cowboy boots, which I knew from experience held a six inch knife tucked inside, and a tank top designed to drive my sexual appetite into a frenzy. When she got dressed she bypassed the bra option. Oh, my. The pony tail was replaced by a Katniss Everdeen braid that would be lethal if she swung her head fast enough.

I tried to avoid commenting on the rain coat draped over Brews six-foot-three frame, so I stared instead. She caught my curiosity and flipped it open to reveal her sculpted body covered by white silk boxing shorts and a white sports bra. I knew she was going to make a fortune in tips, just for the show value. She didn't need confirmation, but asked anyway, "All right with you?"

I'd be a fool to disagree.

Jeanine grabbed a jean jacket and one of those tinkie tiny purse things that was just big enough for her Colt .25 acp Junior. In her rush to the door, she announced, "Norby and I will take his car if it starts, and Brew will drive with Rikki in her pickup. They need to go over the cover Brew's got planned. Lieutenant Grosslein called earlier and said we should stop at the station first."

With that said, we left. Jeanine wrinkled her distaste for my car, "Shit almighty, can't you even clean it?" I had no reasonable answer, so just stared at Brew and Rikki rumbling off in her elevated 4 X 4 Dodge Power Ram. You guessed it; she laid a neat trail of rubber from all four over-sized tires. Jeanine sat back avoiding a touch of anything, except to throw the McDonalds wrappers into the back seat.

At the station, Stu was waiting to go over some logistics of what was going on, and he introduced us to our back-up cop. Unfortunately, it turned out to be officer Darrel Snerd.

Rikki stepped forward and shook his hand. "You were at the crime scene the other day. Glad to meet you."

I wanted to tell her she wasn't glad to meet him.

Stu made certain both Snerd and I were armed, keeping the weapons hidden in the small of our backs, covered by department issued sport coats that had gone out of style with poodle skirts. They smelled like poodles had been sleeping on them and crapping mothballs.

Lieutenant Grosslein looked up at Brew and couldn't close his mouth to talk. He talked too much anyway. I saved his embarrassment, "Stu, you already know Jeanine. This is our partner, Brew. Brew, this is . . ."

She stepped forward grabbing Stu's flabby hand. Her voice was deep and throaty, "I know who he is, bone head." She turned to Snerd, who she obviously was familiar with. "Hi, Darrel. Good to work with you again. It's been awhile, but maybe you're smarter now and won't blow this gig."

Kudos to Brew.

Snerd just stood doing his stupid thing.

She turned back to a mesmerized Stuart Grosslein, explaining, "Snerd and I worked a stake out a long time ago. I used to work CIA undercover, and he was donated by the local force in case we needed a sacrifice. You need to know any more?"

CIA? That earned some respect.

Stu came to life, "Uh, no." Saving his embarrassment, he growled and stomped off to pout. I got the feeling that Lieutenant Grosslein has been left out of the loop on this and was only present because one of his officers was involved. Not including Snerd. Nobody cared about him anyway.

I turned to my esteemed asshole partner, "This is a job, Snerd. Make sure you keep your eyes stuck in your head and watch the crowd. We're going in for a purpose. Its called police work."

Pushing past me, "You ain't even a cop, bone head. I hope they didn't give you bullets for that toy stuck in your belt. Give me a chance, and I'll shove it up your ..."

Rikki, by far the adult here, stepped in actually yelling at both of us. "Stop that, both of you. If you can't act like police officers, stay here and let me do this without breaking up fights between you." Hands planted on her hips, she gave us each ... "the look."

The stern admonition had both me and Snerd feeling like we'd been grounded by mom. The sparks between us were more of a machismo antler rattling, neither willing to give in. Yeah, I know—childish.

The organizing bullshit part was over, so it was time to move. I wondered if Rikki did her John Wayne for Brew. My Reliant rattled into the Conestoga parking lot with Snerd's 2008 Shelby GT500 rumbling behind us. How the hell did he do it? He was a cop. I managed to get the driver's door of the classic Reliant open, albeit with a great amount of squeaking, and stared at the blue-and-white trophy car. If the jerk wasn't beaming with a shit-eaten grin, I'd have complimented him.

My arms open, I stammered, "What, what, what? Where'd you get that?"

He was such a jerk. "I made a drug bust and in return for not cuffing him, he gave me the pink slip. Nice, huh. It's stolen and would get pulled in anyway, so I did him a favor."

Turning in disgust, I looked for Rikki, but she was gone. Stepping in the back door, I encountered Louie. I asked, "Hey, man, did a little blonde gal come in here? She's our waitress plant."

Louie piped up, "Yeah, she said you were in a bitch fight so she came in alone. She's okay, Norbs. Their getting her primed for floor duty. The other gal went to the bar to get scoped in by Pappy. Nice butt on that one."

I was about to warn Louie on the comments that would light Brew's fuse, but figured he could learn the hard way.

I stopped Snerd from getting in the back door, telling him, "We gotta go around front like real customers." In the entry, I pleaded with the asshole, "Please, Snerd, don't get hammered tonight. We're here to protect Officer Thielges. Just this once, please?"

He must have been born with that shit-eaten grin, or it was a facial disorder. "Relax, bone head. I'll be a regular Dick Tracy tonight."

"Yeah, without the Tracy part."

Jeanine, by far smarter than either Snerd or me, strode past us, into the club.

The crowd wasn't too big or noisy yet, and I followed my date to an elevated table near the wall. The first person to make a show was Brew, resplendent in her skimpy outfit. She had a few words with the bartender she'd be working with, got a smiling nod from Louie, and went to work.

Turning to Jeanine, I said, "She looks right at home."

With a knowing grin, "If you'd ever consider not fighting with her all the time you'd discover she has a lot of talents that are very useful." I looked at her thinking that comment could have several meanings.

I craned my neck looking for Snerd, and spotted him trying to pick up a gal I knew as a hooker. I wondered what she'd give him as a favor for not arresting her, besides an STD.

The drinks started flowing and the noise level escalated a few hundred decibels. Traffic on the floor was heavy, so I got serious about being a body guard. The opening act on stage was a duo to get the crowd cranked into a frenzy. Using two kitchen chairs as props, the two young ladies managed to perform acts that would lead to a home invasion by the FCC if it were viewed on the Internet. After an act that suggested sexual satisfaction, they pranced naked around the edge of the stage soliciting donations to be inserted into body cavities one would have to dream about only.

A brief waiting period to let the crowd get wound up again, and then a solo dance by a Cher look-alike. Plying my attention away from Cher, I scanned the crowd for sight of our waitress.

Jeanine poked me with her elbow, and I thought she had broken my ribs. Without pointing, she drew me to a table filled with eight men dressed like Paul

Bunyan. Red flannel shirts, watch caps, and dirty jeans almost reaching the heavy service boots.

She nodded her head, "There she is."

Rikki. Officer Loretta Thielges. Homecoming queen.

It didn't make sense at first. The trays of booze and beer were in an efficient flow from bar to customer, but what I saw wasn't what I wanted to see. Like a giant pipe wrench cranking on my brain, I looked at the crew of misfits and the waitress carrying a tray of beer in pitchers, to wet their whistles, and froze. An, "Oh, my God," dripped out of my mouth and clunked on the floor. "Oh, shit. Oh. Fuck. No." My first thought was the lie I was going to have to tell her father.

The waitresses were topless.

And so was my beloved little Barbie cop. She was dressed exactly like the other five waitresses, in tinkie-tiny red short shorts that almost covered the top half of her little butt, but stopped just short of decently hiding the cleavage that divided the two sides. She was pure flesh from there to the top of her blonde head, and below to the floor. Two perky pink breasts topped by the darker pink areola.

As she leaned over to set the heavy slopping tray on the table, sixteen large calloused hairy hands, complete with dirt encrusted nails, were grabbing like they would come out with fists filled with candy. Her hair had been restyled into two braids like a Swedish milk maid, and they flew in unison to her escape attempt. One of her elbows jabbed the closest man in the nose, toppling him back over the chair, to the floor. In the pause to watch their comrade, Rikki scooted back, with the wet empty tray clutched in her hands as a shield. One other attempt to pull her back into the crowd at the table was answered by the tray being smashed on a thick skull.

I shot off the stool, enraged. About to fly with my red cape fluttering behind me, I was pulled back to the table by someone with more sense than I had. Admonishing my bravado, "Sit down, you ass hole. You're going to blow her cover." Jeanine's fingers were digging into the part of my arm where muscle should have been. "Calm down and watch her work. She's good."

I shot a glance at Brew behind the bar. She was tensed and ready to jump, but held back. I was glad it was Jeanine and not Brew tearing little holes into my arm.

FROM A DARK CORNER AT THE FAR END OF THE BAR, a tall figure lurked in the shadows, watching Norbert Klein with interest. Scanning the activity in the crowded bar, and then a surreptitious exchange with one other person, the satisfied figure turned and disappeared.

CHAPTER
TEN

● ● ● ● ● ● ● ● ● ● ● ● ● ● ● ● ● ● ● ●

TOTALLY DISCOMBOBULATED TO THE POINT of hyperventilating, I sat watching the fray between the tiny blonde waitress and the table full of dock hands. In respect for the mêlée she put up against them, they stood and gave her an appreciative round of applause. Smiling and actually bowing, she raked her tray in a fanning motion, retreating to the kitchen.

In a mock show of adulation, they chanted, "More. More." It got results.

She pranced back into the crowd, the floor clearing in front of her as she made her way back to the goons. In a fluidic gesture she pirouetted and thrust the bill for the beer into the hands of the largest ape in the crowd. As showy and confident as she seemed, I knew she was terrified. Her chest was red from the grappling and abuse, and a red shadow had placed itself on the back of her neck. The goon reached in his pocket and pulled out a wad of bills. Prompting his fellow goons to ante up, Rikki stood still while bundles of cash were crammed into her tiny red shorts. As a final testimony to his respect for the feisty waitress, the big guy planted a hundred dollar bill flat on each breast, holding them in place. With all the grace of a ballet dancer, she slid her little hands under his, bowed, said, "Thank you," and backed away, clutching her reward to her chest.

I was getting sick to the point of barfing, but Jeannine forbid me to do that.

The evening was young with loud and obnoxious assholes wanting more beer and flesh. A full half hour slipped by and Rikki made another appearance. She was a bigger attraction than the professionals on the stage with their legs wrapped around the pole, and each other.

She gave the appearance of being calm and in control. What a lie. I had an idea that she was instructed to concentrate on the same table, which was her destination. The redness on her body had subsided somewhat, and the only difference was a gold barrette clamped into her hair. I knew what the purpose was for that. Hoping it actually worked, it would transmit the garbled and slurred guffaws of eight drunken dock hands to the vigilant ears of the bored feds out in the van.

Taking the order for the next round, she showed more confidence by flirting with a couple of the rowdies. At the bar, Brew filled four iced pitchers with Miller Genuine Draft, adding eight mugs and a clump of napkins. Brew and the mostly naked waitress chatted excitedly, then obviously came to terms, nodding approval for whatever scheme they had.

There was less chaos at the table, and after taking the money and another generous tip, Rikki actually sat on the lap of Paul Bunyan number one. His hands violating every part of bareness, she played into it, performing like a pro.

At 2:00 a.m. one hour after the official Minnesota closing time, Rikki took turns kissing each one of her bums, thanked them, and skipped off into the kitchen.

Jeanine stood up and took a nod from Brew. "Let's go. Rikki's in back." What was with the communication between women? No wonder they made men feel so stupid.

We sauntered out the front door into a deserted Canal Park boardwalk. The dark blue Dodge van sat obscurely in the parking lot, more than likely filled with cigarette smoke, cardboard coffee cups, and bored agents.

The back door was closed, but by the magic of turning the doorknob, it opened for us. There was confusion as we walked through the kitchen, caused by the cleanup crew hoping to get home before the sun rose. Brew, covered with the raincoat, motioned us into a large women's bathroom, and for some reason, the absence of urinals was comical to me.

Rikki sat on a folding metal chair, her head bent forward, resting on her hands, elbows propped on her knees. A woman I never saw before hovered over her gently rubbing her shoulders. The barrette sat on the edge of the sink. Rikki looked up and, seeing us, she pulled a large terry towel over her body, dully staring at the floor.

The strange woman held an air of authority and stood as a protective shield to her charge. Zeroing in on me, the only male in the women's bathroom, and jutted her chin at me. Her order was barked, "You have to leave. She needs to get dressed."

That was the best advice I've heard all day.

Rikki, bone dead tired, stood looking like she just went ten rounds with Laila Ali, the great one's daughter, took a breath and firmly stated, "No, I want him here." When she turned and folded herself into my arms, I was as surprised as I was embarrassed. I wrapped my arms around her and held on tightly, letting her get the sobs out of the way. She looked up, and I kissed the tear running down her cheek.

Quiet and somber, I told her, "Get dressed, honey. I'll take you home."

She gave me a painful smile, nodded and closed herself in the toilet stall. While I waited I glanced around to see if any wanton female had scrawled my name and number on the wall. Nope. I didn't have a marker to add it so I just accepted my anonymity.

Totally oblivious to the crowd in the bathroom, she stripped off the tiny red shorts and tossed them over the partition. Her back pack was slid on the floor in to her and she assembled herself into a state of decency. Opening the door, she looked to the woman who was an agent, and softly made a request. Agent lady left and came back in a moment with a shot glass and a bottle of Canadian Club. She filled it to the brim and passed it to Rikki who unceremoniously tossed it into the back of her throat, she handed the glass back, "More?" Of course, she got it.

Ready to leave, she took my arm, but before getting to the door, the agent asked, "What about all the cash you got?" Her hand swept over the counter by the sink, waving at what must have come to about a grand. Stacks of bills, some neatly assembled, the rest crumpled like old Kleenex—a mute testimony to a job well done tonight.

Rikki gazed at the pile of cash and sneered. "Give it to the Northwood Children's Services. Just don't say where it came from." She grabbed my arm and pulled me outside.

The van was gone, and the small crowd we formed split up to go home. Jeanine offered to stay with Rikki, but she declined. "Thank you, but I just want Norby to take me home." Her voice was slow and dejected.

Brew and Jeanine took off, the Ram Charger rumbling into the darkness of Canal Park and Lake Superior. I creaked open the Reliant's passenger door for her and climbed into my side. Luckily, it started, and smoked its way home.

THE CROWD BEHIND THE CONESTOGA, and the obvious fuss over the blonde waitress, was a tactical blunder, and a potentially fatal one. They had aroused too much attention.

From a dark recess across the parking lot, hidden in the shadows of the tall front of Hell Burger, the commotion created behind the Conestoga Club was being viewed through a Hensoldt night sight scope. One tiny adjustment, and … too late. The group had dispersed and the target was gone. The deadly German Mauser SR-93 sniper rifle was lowered in nervous frustration. A quiet utterance came out, "Damn," slinking back into the void of darkness.

From an obscure position across the street, in the parking lot of the Comfort Suites hotel, the only indication of life was the glow of a cigarette through the windshield of the dark car. The witnessing of the missed opportunity was considered unforgiveable.

CHAPTER
ELEVEN

● ●

Rikki was abnormally quiet all the way to her apartment, but I could feel the tension. Once, she whispered, "What am I going to tell Dad?"

I squealed to a stop in front of the stucco building totally at a loss for words. Looking over I saw a little girl weighted by guilt and shame. She leaned into me and let it all out. In the confines of the front seat, I held her shaking body, whispering what little stupid words of encouragement I could find. The shaking subsided and she pushed away, wiping her face with the too-long sleeves of the sweatshirt.

"Don't leave me alone tonight? Please?"

Not entirely understanding what she meant, upstairs or down here in the car, I would do it. "Sure, honey. I'll stay here."

She cranked the door open, "C'mon up."

I followed closely up to the second floor and waited while she unlocked three deadbolts. Inside, she went straight to the bathroom, not closing the door. I closed my eyes waiting for the vomiting to stop. She flushed and went into the bedroom while I relocked the door and secured two more chains. She had never mentioned a cat, but a large gray one twined itself around my legs getting rid of unwanted hair onto my pants.

I assumed I'd be on the sofa so I sat down waiting. I wanted to help, but I gave her space and stayed out of the way. She would let me know. The bedroom light went out and I wanted to die listening to the sobbing. The most distressing sound I can think of was a woman crying, for real. It just tore me up. Guardedly, I crept into the dark room and put my hand on her shoulder. When she covered mine with hers, I knew I was doing the right thing. I sat on the bed, letting her curl into me, and stroked her hair until the sniffling turned into light snoring. The mangy cat replaced me.

Sleep on the lumpy sofa was not easy to come by, but it smelled better than the sport coat I had been issued. A couple times during the night I was vaguely aware of the toilet being flushed, so she didn't sleep too well either. The cat evidently didn't like to be rousted and spent a more peaceful night sleeping on my head.

Daylight and I forced myself upright. The apartment was deadly still, and I wondered if she was even here. In my stocking feet, I crept to her door and peeked in at the small lump huddled in the center of a queen-size bed. I pulled the door shut forcing myself to be quiet, and went into the kitchen to experiment with making coffee. I hoped she wasn't a tea drinker. I hate that stuff. I also hate the foo-foo barf-a-rama with the French names that were coffee substitutes. I was afraid to dig too deep into the cupboard, for fear of making noise, and giving the impression I was snooping.

I heard the toilet flush again and she presented herself. Her body was draped with a cotton sleeveless light blue gown that stopped just above her knees. She was barefoot. My smile was meant to be warming, "I can't find the coffee." My lips were straining to look jovial.

The look on her face was a dark scowl, framed by a wild mass of blonde hair that was out of control. Stomping to a cupboard I had neglected to open, she reached in and handed me a tin of Maxwell House. I didn't dare ask for a coffee pot. Her bedroom door slammed shut, opened again, followed by the bathroom door slamming shut.

The noise from the running shower gave me cover to look deeper for a coffee pot. Aha! An old Mr. Coffee dating back to the sixties was crammed into a back corner. Using my adaptive skills as a seasoned investigator, I managed to construct a coffee project. There was only one way to plug it in, so I was okay there, and then became smart enough to punch the magic red button.

She came traipsing out of the bathroom followed by a wall of steam, and slammed the bedroom door again. Under normal circumstances she would have never allowed me to see her wrapped in a bath towel, and out of respect I looked away anyhow. Too much had happened and there was a lot of healing to do. If I was anything, now, I needed to be understanding. I also needed to feed the cat.

She emerged from the bedroom in a better mood and didn't punish the door any more. The jeans were tattered and faded, and a too long blue flannel shirt turned her into the little girl I loved like a father. The wet mop of blonde had been combed into neat rows across her head, to hang down her back.

I sat on the sofa with my cup of excellent coffee, hoping I would never be asked to make another one. This pot was an experiment I could never duplicate. She poured herself one into a big ceramic mug she held in both hands. There was a picture of Garfield on the side of the cup. Sniffing the fragrance, she started becoming human again.

Sitting next to me, she stared and spoke into the mug. "I'm sorry for acting like a jerk this morning. You've been so helpful and I treated you like shit."

"I'm used to it. How are you?"

"I don't have an answer for that yet. I don't know." She looked up at me, "I'm so ashamed of what I did and what people saw, I can't think straight."

"You're looking at it from the wrong side. Yes, you were naked in front of a crowd of morons and everyone saw you. I can only imagine the fear and embarrassment you felt. However, believe it or not, you are a hero. You wanted to be respected as a good cop, and now you have paid your dues and earned your place in the hierarchy of the good old boys club. You will be remembered for being brave."

That infectious smile again. "Thanks, Norby. But still, what do I tell Dad?"

"He loves you and details about stuff that'll make him uncomfortable will serve no purpose. Leave it alone. He's a smart guy and will learn what he needs to know in time. No matter what, you'll never be seen any differently by him. Or me."

"Thanks, Norby. I'm starved and I don't have anything edible here. Let's go out for breakfast."

"If you let me buy, I know just the place."

Settled in the Reliant, my prayer was answered, and it started. Pulling away, I commented, "So, you going to tell the chief you're done with this gig now?"

Startled, she glared at me, "Done? Hell, no. I'm going to finish this. Getting naked for the entire city of Duluth is not going to be my legacy. I still need to get them to talk about the shipping or whatever it is that's happening on the pier."

Her determination was grinding on me, but I was so proud of her.

Hell Burger was just across the parking lot from the Conestoga Club. The Reliant dieseled itself to a shut-down mode, and when the smoke cleared Rikki creaked open the car door and stepped to the pavement. I caught the hesitation on her face as she stared at the massive structure across the parking lot that she hated so much. "You okay, Rikki?"

"Yeah, I'm fine. Just don't talk about it, okay?"

I sidled past the remains of Angie, still decorating the parking lot, and stepped into the darkness of Hell Burger. I waved to Pappy, behind the bar, "Hey, man, why so dark in here?"

His comment made perfect sense. "'Cause we're closed, bone head."

Dumb as a mud fence, the only intelligent answer I had was, "Oh."

He waved his bar rag directing us. "In the back. Kitchens open. Just don't let Mitch know you're here."

Rikki, by far the brighter of the two of us, led me to the rear into the busy kitchen. Accosted at the door, we were facing the pleasant smile of Brian Melland. Rikki took on the shade of a good sunburn and became speechless.

There was something drastically wrong with his presentation, and I was compelled to ask, "Brian, why are you wearing pajamas?"

He looked down at the blue flannel covered with lambs, "I dunno. Something Mitch has dreamed up for a party tonight."

Far from being embarrassed by another hair-brained scheme by his boss, he was more concerned with my little partner. "Hi, Loretta." As an afterthought, without looking at me I at least got a, "Hi, Norby."

Since Rikki was busy turning white again, I asked, "Any place we can roost and get a breakfast?"

Calm and suave, Brian assured us we were going to get fed. "Sure, this way." He led us into Mitch's office and cleared the crap off the top of his desk. "There's some stuff being cooked I'll bring in." Once again, the shit-eating grin. "Hi, Loretta."

Moments later, Brian came back with a tray of hash browns, scrambled eggs, sausage links, and coffee. "Well now, this should work for you." Side-stepping an invitation he sat down next to Rikki. "Hi, Loretta."

Shoving hash browns into her face, she mumbled, "You already said that, Brian."

Aware of his fascination for Rikki, and disturbed by the swift assembly of breakfast, I asked, "This was pretty quick service, Brian. You make this up ahead of time?"

His eyes still locked onto Rikki's baby blues, he smiled his answer, "Yeah. They were cooked up for Mitch. He worked late last night and slept upstairs. He's up there waiting for it."

Oh, shit.

"Brian, we're eating Mitch's breakfast?"

"That's okay. They're cooking up another one."

Oh, shit.

Busy passing school-kid glances at each other, Rikki took charge, "Well, thank you, Brian. That was the best stolen breakfast I've had today."

The hapless young man reached into the perennial bowl of M&M's always in sight on Mitch's desk, handing Rikki a green one. Her smile spread across her face, which had returned to white-girl shade again. "Thank you, Brian." I took note of her clutching it in the palm of her hand.

Anxious to get out of there before Mitch found out I ate his breakfast, I prodded Rikki to say goodbye to her attraction. A last ditch effort to make a connection, Brian asked, "Can I call you sometime?"

Oh, man, the guy was smitten.

I watched as every ounce of essence drained from her, sinking her deeper than she needed to go. She reached out to touch his arm, "I'll let you know. Thanks for the M&M."

Back into the Plymouth, her sleeve blotted the tear. Looking at me, she wailed, "He's going to find out."

"He's head over heals for you. He's compassionate enough to understand what happened, and why. Don't shut him off."

The starter motor in the Reliant clicked instead of whining. By experience, I knew I needed to wait a moment. Rikki was scanning the Conestoga building while the Plymouth made up its mind on whether or not to start. "Why do they do it?"

"Huh? Do what and who?"

"The strippers. Every night they dance naked in front of perverts. What's in their heads to allow that to happen?"

"The need to earn a living. Most of the girls are students at UMD. Others are mothers with abusive husbands either stoned or in jail." I wondered where Clete Michaels was.

I thanked the Reliant for starting and left, Rikki still wondering about the girls who called the stage and pole their office.

Pulling to the curb at her apartment building, she said, "Thanks, Norby. I have to change and go see Lieutenant Grosslein, then get trained on my new computer. Will you be there tonight?"

It took a moment to answer because I couldn't think of a way to convince her to not show up. "Yeah. I'll be there with Jeanine and Brew."

I noticed she was toying with her green M&M. "That's supposed to melt in your mouth, not your hand. You going to eat it?"

The smile came back, yet abashed at my suggestion, "I can't eat it. He gave it to me. Isn't he cute?"

I knew the piece of candy would be put in her jewelry box to be kept forever. "You want me to pick you up?"

She put on her business-like attitude to tell me she was old enough to take care of herself. "Not this time. I'm going to drive myself, but I need to know you're going to be there."

"We'll all be there. I want to check with the monkeys in the surveillance van to see how it's going on their end. Don't worry about anybody but yourself."

She gave me a quick, "See ya, be ya," and hopped out. When I was sure she wasn't beamed into space by evil forces, I coaxed the Plymouth to go home.

It was a foregone conclusion that I was a bumbling idiot. I'd never denied that. The underlying fact of why I was still alive rested with that little bell that sent a signal to the pit of my stomach when the meat wasn't really kosher. I couldn't count the times I'd stopped in my tracks to see what was going on with that little warning, and lived because of it.

It was dinging now. Something was wrong and I'd never been so scared in my life.

It was just noon and way too early for my spook Hanky to come out of his hole. I hung around the vacant appliance store that housed my apartment, but to no avail.

When it was time for Hanky to join his own level of society, I'd be at the Conestoga Club.

Kathleen Pierpont was close—I could feel it. The hair on the back of my neck bristled and if I was still alive it was because she had something special waiting for me.

CHAPTER
TWELVE

● ●

TRYING TO DECIDE IF I SHOULD GET DRUNK, get laid, or both, my reverie was interrupted by the flashing lights of a patrol car that had snuck up behind me. My brain tried to process enough information on why I was targeted, but it was asleep. Duh. I was sitting in the open street waiting for a lunatic to murder me, and I couldn't think fast enough to conjure up a lie to a cop.

As involved as much as I was with the police, it was always frightening when a cop approached, and I didn't know why. The bulky blue leaned on the window frame of the Reliant, "Hey, Norbs, what's cookin'?"

Luckily, it was a cop I knew fairly well and couldn't think of any reason he would have a distaste for me. I pissed off a lot of cops, so providence was on my side. I thought. "Oh, hey, Mike. You gave me a start. What'd I do wrong this time?"

"I dunno, Norby. Did you do something wrong?"

Cat and mouse game. "I got out of bed this morning. That's the worst so far. What's with you?"

He stood up, stretching, and then came back to my level. I could swear I smelled a tinge of booze on his breath, but I'd be an even bigger dope to bring it up. In my days as a cop, having a slug of hootch was the best way to stay level. "The lieutenant told me to find you. Seems you have an appointment with the shrink. If it's the one I think it is, I'd turn on the lights and siren to get there sooner. He wants to make sure you don't miss it. If you ain't gonna show up, can I take your place?"

I smiled at that and wished I could make it happen. "I don't think so, Mike. The good Dr. LaRioux has this thing for me. She wants me."

He chuckled, "Yeah, I see what you mean."

He had something else on his mind but wasn't sure he should say something. I saved him the trouble. "Spit it out, Mike. What's got you tied up? Go ahead, talk open with me."

He hesitated, then slowly drew out, "Well, there's some talk that you're hiding some shit and a whole bunch of people want it. You've always been straight with me, Norby, so I'd hate to see you get hurt for something that might not even be true."

More cat and mouse. He'd been told to go fishing by the chief. "Mike, you know about rumors in a squad room. People like to toss them around when they can't think of anything intelligent to say. Just talk, Mike. I'm not hiding anything."

"That's cool. I believe you."

Under normal circumstances, that would be enough to get him to walk away. He was still fishing. "One other thing, Norby. Is it true that Pierpont dame is on the loose?"

Now, that stung. "The lieutenant tell you to bring that up?"

He didn't offer an answer, but that was as good as one. He stood up, patted the window frame a couple times, and said, "Don't forget to see the shrink. I'm supposed to follow you to make sure you really do it."

"Baby sitter?"

He tossed his arms in the air in the universal sign of, I dunno.

The only place to park that was reasonably close to the shrink's office was a no parking zone. I pulled in anyway. Mike pulled his war wagon along side, got out, and stuck a Police Vehicle sign under my tattered windshield wiper blade. I saw him look at the rubber hanging from the wiper and shake his head. He gave me the thumbs up sign and left.

She had been watching me approach her office, because before I could even knock, the door swung open. She cooed, "Mr. Klein, I wasn't sure you'd show up today. Please, come in."

The inside of Doctor Ariel LaRouix's office was freezing cold. I think that's to control the raging sexual heat emanating from her body. Today, she dressed special for me. A sleeveless tight silk blouse and a skirt that was three inches too short. She walked around in her bare feet and each step she took made her calves do amazing tricks.

"I chose this over being arrested."

Her head tilted in a quizzical gesture that had way too many connotations attached to it. "Hmmm?"

I didn't know if I should get undressed now, or wait to be ordered.

I took my spot on the tiny sofa, and she perched her marvelous round butt on her doctor chair. The too short skirt pulled up when she crossed her legs, and I figured there was about an eighth of an inch from the hem of the skirt to her magic garden. She bypassed the clipboard prop this time. Her lips pursed and I knew she was going to breathe some kind of sound from them. "So, Mr. Klein, how have you been? Any more delusions on someone trying to kill you?"

My tongue was too hard to allow me to speak. "Uh, um, okay, yup."

She paraded her sexuality around me for another half hour, until I had to stop her. If I sat here any longer watching her use her softness and cleavage to wear me down, I'd have an explosion in my pants. I was far too human to sustain any more. I'd rather be water-boarded. I wanted to stand up and leave, but I couldn't. So, I did the next best thing that I did. I became an asshole.

While she was breathing words to me, I put my hand up, "Stop. Please. Ariel—I can call you Ariel, can't I? Look, this party has gone too far. I'd like to sit here all night and ogle your curves, watching you manipulate your softness to get me to talk, but I have someplace to be soon, which is far more important than fantasizing about having sex with you. You've been told to hypnotize me to tell you where I've hidden some bonds. Well, you can strip down to all flesh if you want, but I'll tell you, there are no bonds. Not that I wouldn't want to watch you do a strip, but, you can tell the lieutenant that I have nothing for you. Or him. While you're wasting time seducing me, Kathleen Pierpont is planning on killing me."

My jabbering had an effect on my blood flow, and I discovered I could stand without broadcasting my desire. "So, unless you're going to do a quick strip for free, I gotta go."

She sat still on her doctor chair, and quit talking, but kept her lips parted slightly. "You are too transparent, Mr. Klein. You'll be back, I'm certain of that." She finally stood up, shifting the patch of skirt, "You are far from being an enticing man, Norbert, and I find you distasteful in so many ways." Knowing she was the master and I was the slave, she stepped to me, put both hands on my shoulders, and kissed me on the lips. "For your home work, think about my stripping and having sex with you. Would that get you to come back?"

My eyeballs were going to fry in the sockets. Her lips were small, wet, and burning. If she had tied strings to my hands and feet, turning me into a mindless marionette, I'd let her. Then I'd hang in her toy box until the next time. I managed to save my dignity by saying, "Uh, um, oh, ah, hm. Yeah. Okay."

She twisted me around to face the door, "Goodbye, Mr. Klein. You don't need an appointment next time."

The door closed behind me and I stood still until the shaking stopped. It was getting late, and although my brain was still in a fog, I managed to find my Plymouth. Sitting on top of the POLICE VEHICLE sign was a parking ticket.

CHAPTER
THIRTEEN

R IKKI'S MUSTANG WAS PARKED BEHIND THE CONESTOGA CLUB. The hood was still warm, so I could guess when she got here. Brew's Ram Charger was parked far enough away not to be considered part of the Conestoga crowd. I hoped Jeanine was with her. I went in the front door, paid the cover, and scouted for Jeanine. Brew was behind the bar wearing a black sports bra and tight fitting shorts that looked like the bottom of a sexy swim suit. I have to admit, the girl was one amazing display of sex. I waved but she ignored me. I got that a lot.

Scanning the tables for my date, I spied her in a back corner talking to some guy in a leather sports coat. I could imagine he drove a Beemer. He was laying over the table, trying to consume Jeanine with his suave manner. I didn't worry about her, knowing her capabilities. If he went too far, she could embarrass him, break some bones, slit his gut open, or shoot him. Yes, she was proficient in doing all of that, and those were the milder forms of torment she was rated expert in.

I shuffled through the crowd, getting some rude comments in doing so, and approached the table. With a bright smile, I blurted out, "Hi, honey. Sorry I'm late, but the kids wanted to say goodnight to you."

The show-off dude got upset, but all I got from Jeanine was a dry uninterested look. She understood what I was doing and played her part smoothly, though. "Hi, honey. This is Warren. Warren, meet my husband, Clyde. Warren's an entrepreneur, sweetie." She put her hand on Warren's shoulder, "Warren, my husband Clyde harvests worms. He's a wormologist. A Ph.D. no less."

I reached out to Warren but only got a fistful of air to shake. "Helminthologist, sweetums. And, they aren't just worms, they are helminths. You never do get that right, do you? Warren, would you be a dear and call our babysitter?"

Warren's sneer was too much. He mumbled something, but fortunately, we missed it. I sat down and took a drink of the stuff sitting in front of Jeanine.

"Ohph, what the hell is that?" I looked for a place to spit it out, but swallowed instead.

She recaptured her drink, telling me, "Warren bought that. It's called a slow screw. I think he had similar thoughts."

"Hm, I guess I came in too soon." I scanned the floor, but didn't see Rikki. "Is she here?"

"Yeah. She won't be coming out until later when the crowd gets thicker."

"Jeanine, is she going to make it through a whole night?"

"She's a big girl, Norbs. Give her some credit. We'll keep tabs on her." She pushed her empty glass at me and said, "Some husband you are. Get me another drink. Only this time I'll have a beer."

I got two Miller Light, on tap, from Brew, and she made me pay for my own. I sneered at her, and she gave me the finger. I saw that she was giving the floor a good watch to get an idea of where the trouble might start. In spite of her hatred for me, I was glad she was there. I started to fantasize about doing her in the rack, but Doctor LaRioux's image crowded her out.

About three beers each later, a new crowd came in. The dock workers. They cleared some drunks and college kids out of four tables, pushed them together, and staked their claim. A few minutes later, my little girl made an appearance, and I went into shell shock again. I expected the topless, as that was the attraction last night, but this time, her uniform had been modified. The girls were wearing bright orange thongs along with the nothing on their boobs. Not much material was wasted in them, a small patch in the front at the crotch, and a tiny string around the hips and down through the butt canyon.

Oh shit!

The night wore on with Rikki taking center stage again. Some jerk offered her a hundred dollars for the orange piece of crotch string, but she just took the money and laughed it off. The guy was pleased for the attention, anyway.

Dragging on towards 2:00 a.m., and the crowd oozed out the door. I expected a repeat of last night, and Jeanine and I went to the ladies room off the kitchen to get our girl. All we found in there was a cook shooting up some coke. "Where's the girl? The blonde?"

He gave us a blank smile and wheezed out, "Hey, man."

We ran out front and collared Louie. "Hey, hairy man, where's Rikki?"

He had no idea. The next stop in our race with panic was to the stake-out van outside. We banged on the door, and it was opened by a girl pulling her blouse back over her boobs. "Oh, swell."

Jeanine was first in the van, yelling, "Where's the Thielges girl? The under-cover you're supposed to be watching?"

Zipping up his fly, he said, "That never went down. We were told to not worry about listening to her. There wasn't much from last night, so tonight was can-celled."

It was my turn to yell, "So what the hell were you doing out here?"

He looked after the girl who had stepped outside to adjust her jeans, and said with a grin, "What else?"

"You dumb jackass. That girl put her life on the line for evidence and you sit out here fucking teenagers?" He couldn't understand what he had done wrong, so when my fist slammed into his face, he was really surprised. He shook the blood off, staggered up and lunged at me, growling.

He would have killed me if he hadn't run into the barrel of Jeanine's nine-mil. She followed with a snide, "Move one inch and you fucking die, maggot."

That, he understood. He backed off. Jeanine, by far the most organized and smartest here, asked, "Okay, shit head; you were told the surveillance was off. By who?"

He sniffled in some nose blood, and whispered, "I don't know."

She pointed the nine-mil at the floor and a slug split the wood near his foot. "Not the right answer."

He jumped back, "Oh, shit. Don't do that, lady."

She stepped to him, placed the muzzle against his forehead, and said, quietly, "Who gave the order?"

He recoiled at the heat from the muzzle, and stammered, "I don't know. We got a call on the cell phone. That's all we knew. Honest."

She held out her hand. "Give me the phone."

"Yeah, sure. Here." He picked up the tiny phone from the counter top and handed it over.

That led nowhere, and I was first out the door, but was surprised by the noise from Jeanine's boot heel smashing into the guy's chest. He flew back and lay crumpled on the floor, his back against the far wall. She marched past me, mumbling, "Prick."

The unmistakable rumble of Brews Ram Charger filled the air, and if hadn't moved, she would have put mudder tracks along my body. She hung out the open door, calling out, "Did you find her?"

Jeanine ran to the passenger side, yelling back, "No, get us to the office, fast."

Watching the big red muscle truck launch itself from the parking lot, I had to think that my status here was really minuscule. Calling to nobody, "Hey, wait for me."

I ran to the back of the Conestoga Club. The Mustang was gone. Well, for lack of any other feeling, I thought that might be a good thing. Hopefully, she went home. But in reality, I knew better.

I banged on her apartment door, and then called. I heard the phone inside ringing. And ringing. She wasn't there. On a last ditch hunch, I raced to Sy's house. Maybe she went to see her dad. God, I hope she changed first. He just wouldn't understand her costume. The Mustang was nowhere in sight. She had disappeared. The time element from the end of the last call, to when we ran out to the van, was no more than a minute. This was bad.

My last option was Pink Power Investigations. If they'd let me in. I was beginning to feel unwanted. Brew's monster truck was out front, and there were lights on inside. The door was locked, and I didn't dare bang on it to get them to let me in. Instead, I proved what a cunning investigator I really was. I used my key to unlock it.

The two girls, well, Jeanine was one girl, and I hadn't figured out about classifying Brew yet—female was as close as I could get, but I haven't seen any physical proof—were sitting at one of the desks staring at the cell phone Jeanine had commandeered.

I spoke before they could yell at me to get out. "Any trace on the origination of the call to the van?"

Since Brew thought I was a leper, Jeanine fielded my concern. "No, it was blocked."

I still had some investigative cunning, telling them, "I'm going to the station and issue an APB for her car. It was gone from the parking lot. If it's not in a garage it'll be easy to spot."

Evidently, Brew had something to offer. "Look, bone head, why don't you get lost and let us . . ."

I realize I'm not regarded with a lot of respect, and I deserve most of that. However, her attitude and comment, at this particular time, sent my blood through a percolator, reaching the boil level very quickly. I didn't care if she was frightening. The confrontation she was forcing on me, as worried as I was about Rikki, hit the fan. My outburst went an octave louder than anybody expected.

"Goddamit, Brew, just shut the fuck up. I'm tired of fencing with you, wondering when you're going to try proving you're a better man than anyone else. I don't give a rat's ass what you think, and if you get in my way of finding Rikki, I'm going to blow your goddamn brains out."

In an incredibly stupid move, I stepped to her and went on yelling. "I'm involved here as much as you. I paid my dues a long time ago, and if you don't like it, I don't give a shit."

I never saw it happen but the next thing I knew I was laying on the floor with a bloody nose. And in a move that surprised even me, I drew my .38 out of the shoulder holster, aimed it at her, and squeezed the trigger. The slug slammed into her shoulder, and I pulled the hammer back to plant one in her head. I'd never been so pissed and never thought about what I was doing. Fortunately, Jeanine jumped and slapped my hand as soon as I fired. The slug grazed Brews head through the hair line.

Brew stepped back, stunned. She looked down at the splotch of red spreading over her chest, and brought her gaze up to me, blood puddling on her forehead. I got to my feet and knew I was going to kill her. Raising the .38, I staggered to her to finish. I heard Jeanine screaming, but it was an echo. Rikki was missing and this piece of shit in front of me wasn't doing enough to find her. I was going to kill her then go look for Rikki.

But, I couldn't. Jeanine was standing in front of me, her hands on my shoulders holding me back. I didn't realize she had taken my gun away. Then, the plug was pulled, and my emotions swirled down the drain. I was done. Brew would live and I would hate her.

The chaos in the Pink Power office was too much. Screaming, pushing, excitement, confusion, and I walked out. The Reliant knew where I lived and did something to make certain that I got there without hurting anybody. Like a faithful horse that always did the right thing, or a dog that could talk and heal. Like a car that usually started at the most critical times.

My hovel was dark and dirty, but it was home. My refuge where I could sit alone and regret what I had just done to Brew—and to Cheryl, Marci, and Laura. I don't remember ever consciously spending fifty-dollars on a big bottle of Jack Daniels, but I had one. Somehow. Maybe the Reliant stopped and got it for me on the way home. I had it and I was going to pour it all down my throat in an alcoholic kamikaze dive.

I didn't have much in the way of furniture, the floor being not only the most comfortable, but the closest, thing to sit on. So, I sat and drank, thinking death this way was less painful than a bullet, or Kathleen's knife across my throat. I had enough fortitude to get off the floor and use the bathroom when needed, but got back to sitting on the floor again. Once in a while I'd sit on the bed, listen to the springs squeak, then go back to the floor and listen to myself cry.

Rikki was gone and I was too fucked up to look for her.

There was no way to gauge how long I stewed, but my closest guess was forever. It got light out, then dark again. Several times. When my brain was working it forced me to look at life and where I was parked in it. I went all the way back to my wife, Cheryl, and how badly I treated her. Then I tortured myself more over Marci Hudson, who was smarter than I was and stayed away from me. The worst was Laura. She was murdered right here in this apartment by Kathleen Pierpont. I thought about the old Norbert Klein Detective Agency when Jeanine and I were partners and solved a lot of problems for paying customers. The good old days.

Daylight had traded places with darkness a few more times and I was still fucked up. I had to find Rikki. I had to find my feet. I had to stop the pounding noise. Pounding noise? There was a woodpecker on my front door. Tap, tap, tap. I hate birds. I screamed at the noise, "Get out. Fly away."

My hand had cramped onto the neck of the Jack Daniels bottle and I couldn't put it down. Some son of a bitch was knocking on my door. I had hopes it was Mrs. Feldstein, my adoptive Jewish mother from down the hall. She could work wonders with chicken soup, and had even taken bullets out of my body. I still didn't understand the concept of kosher bacon, but she did it. She was my saint-in-charge when Kathleen was murdering Laura. She warned me, but I was too stupid to listen. I was no better now. I was still stupid, and I wanted that door knocking to stop.

I opened my mouth to scream another threatening order, but I couldn't get enough wind to push it out. The thought ran through my mush that it may be Kathleen coming in to finish her project of killing me. My only weapon was a half empty huge bottle of good booze. I could get her drunk and overpower her. Yeah.

I was struggling to get my feet to be at the bottom of my body, wrenching myself into an upright defensive position. Shit. The door slowly swung open and I wished it was Kathleen Pierpont instead. The door opening was filled with the muscular frame of my arch enemy who I had failed to kill, when was it? How many nights ago? Shit. Muscle upon muscle rippled on the massive frame of an amazon who hated me almost as much as I hated her. The left arm was in a sling, and the right one hung at her side, with a gun saddled in it. Shit.

I was ready for a paranormal rush of fire gushing from her mouth to singe me into charcoal. One giant step and she was inside. Shit. I hope it was quick because I was a spineless coward. She spoke and the mellow tone was out of place when I expected a flame thrower instead. "Mind if I come in?"

"Shoot me from there. You can get away faster." I sounded like a pubescent kid, croaking my words. She came to me, and I tried to remember how to cringe. The hand with the gun came up, and my life flashed before my bloodshot eyes. She held it out, butt first, "You left this at the office. You might need it."

My answer, "Could you shoot yourself? I'm not in very good shape right now."

She smiled. I wondered what that meant. "We need to talk. Jeanine said so, and I think it's a good idea."

I had managed to sit on the squeaky mattress, still hanging on to the bottle. I offered a conciliatory gift, "Want a drink?"

"Sure." She wrenched the bottle out of my hand, and my fingers went into a spasm. The gun slipped out my other hand and clunked on the floor.

She ingested about a pint of Jack and didn't even wheeze. She handed it back and I slurped some more. Girl germs.

"Norby, I came to offer you an apology."

Maybe I wasn't drunk enough. I was hearing strange words. "Apology? Why? For real?"

"Yeah, for real. I was totally wrong the other night, and I don't blame you for shooting me. Reverse the roles, and I would have shot you. I would've done a better job though." Another smile.

I pondered this for a moment, "You aren't going to kick me out the window?"

She reached out and checked the dried blood on my face. "I'm glad I didn't break your nose."

"So that's what bled so much."

She smiled, took the bottle and poured more into her mouth. Man. "Sorry. Norby, I really want to work with you. Jeanine told me stuff all about you and I saw that you are a decent guy. I got defensive thinking I was going to lose Jeanine because of you. Well, she made it clear that while she was bi-sexual, all we were going to share was an occasional romp. That's fine. As long as I know. I'm a flaming dyke and we people just seem to get possessive."

I had nothing to add to that, or counter it in any way. My turn to lament, "When we first opened the agency I put a move on Jeanine, and she put me in the hospital. My first lesson in learning boundaries. We have, or had, a good relationship and were able to do a lot together. We've helped a lot of people, and put some in jail, and even ended a few snaky lives. We work together. That's all. I love her like a sister and will protect her as much as she'll let me. Nice ass, but too fussy to lower herself to my level."

We sucked on the bottle some more before she got into her personal life. "I was gang raped at an early age. Twelve. I went through a lot of emotions to find a better place after it happened, but what really worked was revenge. About a year later, I had managed to castrate all but one of them. The last one just, uhm, just went away. Enough said about that. I got into martial arts and body building as a defense. I became a cop in a little town in Michigan, then found an application for the CIA. I was an agent for seven years, a lot of undercover vice and stuff. My cover was blown so I got out. I met Jeanine a few years ago and we took to each other. When you were in the hospital from what the Pierpont dame did to you, she called me to help her get her own agency going. I don't know how long I'll hang on here, but before I leave I'd like to help put the Pierpont bitch away. And,

I want to help with Rikki. I know what she's doing, but she's out of her league. She needs to get out. I want to help you find her. Will you let me?"

Brew was looking more into me than at me and I was touched by her sincerity. As long as she wasn't going to break my bones, I thought I could learn to tolerate her. Trust would come later. "Sure, Brew, I'd like to have you help."

I've never been known as an eloquent speaker, or even a polite one. Why change now? "Brew, I'm curious. Where'd you get the name?"

"My parents were Swedish and I was born just as they got off the boat at Ellis Island. My full name was Brusella, but it got shortened real quick. Not much better than Norbert, is it?"

She stood up, drained the fifty-dollar bottle of Jack, and reiterated our working together. "So, are we partners? No bad blood, even on your face? Or my head and shoulder?"

"I like that better than us trying to kill each other. What did you tell the hospital about the gunshot wound?"

"I avoid hospitals. Especially with gunshot wounds. I know some people that do the job with no advertising."

I was curious. "You've been shot before?"

Almost as proud as showing off a tattoo, she asked, "Want to see?"

"Uh, yeah, I guess." The next act floored me.

She unthreaded the sling and took off all of her clothing. Oh, my, God. This was way better than my picture of Brooklyn Decker. In a masterful display of striptease, she shed everything, down to her finely tuned torso. With no concern for my gaping, she pointed to seven spots, explaining each one. "See, here, and here and oh, this one really pissed me off." On the side of her right breast was a small lesion. She bent closer, asking me, "Touch it. It's numb."

"Ah, uhm, I'm not sure I should touch anything."

Her smile spread across the room, "You embarrassed? Come on, Norby, take it. I'm giving a one time offer. Never again, man."

Oh, shit. "You sure?"

"You know, one of my undercover gigs was a porno operation. I posed and did guys in every way you could imagine."

Me, being dumb, "Huh?"

"It became so routine I couldn't think of it as sex any more."

Well, with a naked amazon standing in front of me, what do you expect me to do. So much for my portrayal of same sex partnerships. Yup, and it was one bodacious trip that I'll never forget. Man. Strictly routine for her, but a wild ride for me. Finally done, I lay panting, and told her, "Awesome for a lesbian. Are all of you gals gifted like that?"

She grabbed my manhood, twisted it unmercifully, and told me, "Get dressed, and if you ever want to do that again, it will be in your dreams. Come on, we have to find Rikki."

CHAPTER
FOURTEEN

● ● ● ● ● ● ● ● ● ● ● ● ● ● ● ● ● ● ● ●

Brew rumbled off in the Ram Charger to tell Jeanine what plan A was, although I wasn't aware of any plan. I'll let the two of them sort it out. If Amazonia tells Jeanine about our escapade, she'll likely toss my egg-crate desk outside. For Brew to come to me with conciliatory offerings, was either an agreement with Jeanine, or a deeper plan to offset me for a final disposal. While the romp was enjoyable, it was probably a mistake. I just hoped Rikki shows up before plan B unfolded.

I stopped at the Department of Motor Vehicles to register her car as stolen. If she was just driving around in it, I thought I could weather her storm on being stopped. She was a cop. She'd handle it. Next, I dropped in to see my lifelong pal, Detective Lieutenant Stuart Grosslein. After high school, we parted ways for a while, me into the Army, and Grossy swallowed up by the Marines. I was a grunt adept at crawling through mud and killing short oriental soldiers. Grossy got into something he never talked about, so I left his military past alone.

Vietnam was a sad, confusing time in a lot of lives. It made no sense to calculate who was winning by the number of dead at the end of the day. The exact number was ambiguous——the VC not being able to count too well, and the US lying to slant the results for good press.

My business today was to put out a missing person report on Officer Loretta Thielges. I caught Stu in his office with his finger up his nose, bursting in quickly enough to embarrass him. "Damn it, Klein, can't you knock first?"

"Don't fret, Grossy, you usually have your finger up your ass. It's good to see you varying your posture once in a while."

"What do you want, asshole?"

"Rikki's missing and we can't find any trace of her car. She disappeared after the Conestoga closed up on Saturday. Have you put out a watch for her?"

He sat down, wiping his finger on his pants. "Yeah, we know she's gone, but we're not going to put out an APB yet. If she's with the dock gang, then she's trying to infiltrate and will get hold of us."

Now my juices were starting to heat up. "You aren't even looking for her?"

"Relax, Klein. Yes, we're looking, but we have to keep the interest down so nobody fingers her as a plant."

We argued for about a half hour, and I came out convinced that while still precarious, she wasn't forgotten. Far from comforting. I had a couple cups of precinct coffee often mistaken for diarrhea, and got up to leave. Stu stopped me at the door, "Hey, Norby, we're having a barbecue at the house on Sunday. Why don't you drop by and share a beer."

I hadn't seen Stu's family for almost a year, and wondered if they had all left him.

His wife, Noreen, was a kind, plumpy type, who always made me feel welcome. Except for when I barfed on her new carpet. In spite of being from Stu's loins, his daughter, Isabelle, was a chubby high school junior with a permanent acne attack looking for a way to get pregnant to shock her parents. I suggested setting fire to the house instead, but she didn't want to wreck anything. My logic on a house being temporarily wrecked, against her life being wrecked forever, made no sense to her. Fortunately, her physical appearance and a hostile attitude kept her womb free from invasion.

Getting over the shock of being accepted socially, I answered, "Sure. Maybe I'll bring Jeanine's partner, Bruin Heinz. Just hide the whiskey."

He stood up, "Uh, Norby, maybe not. Okay?"

"Something wrong with her? She scare you too?"

"No. No, not a bit. Just come alone, okay?"

Quizzically, I answered, "Sure. No date. See you Sunday." At the door, I asked, "By the way, what day is today?"

He snapped back, "Wednesday. What's the matter with you?"

"Just asking. Thanks."

Back in the Reliant, I just sat wondering what to do next. I had never felt so helpless not knowing where to turn. My only option left was to go back to the Conestoga and talk to as many as possible to see if they saw Rikki on Saturday night.

Wednesday night was not a particularly busy night in a strip club, so the crowd was sparse. I sat in the women's dressing room prying the minds of naked ladies stoned into another time zone. Most remembered seeing Rikki at the busy dock workers table, but knew nothing after that. Damn.

Nobody at the Hell Burger saw her either. Dejected and confused, I stepped into the evening and saw a group of the dock workers pile into the Conestoga. Finally, an electric current zapped through my brain and I had a course of action set. Rikki had been catering to them, so they were the closest connection. I sat in the Plymouth churning all the details I could remember into items I could logically look at. Its called organizing, and I'm terrible at it.

About midnight, my head had been flopping back and forth, in and out of sleep, giving me a piercing pain in my neck. It hit the head rest with a clump, jolting me awake. "Oh, shit. I gotta stay awake." I began pinching my inside thigh in a tender spot, bringing tears to my eyes. Almost certain that I felt blood running down my leg from the abuse, I stopped to consider that I had peed in my pants. Checking, that wasn't it, but I really did have to take a leak. The small crowd in the Conestoga would probably stay in place for at least another hour, so I slid out of the car, to take care of my problem. Standing at the side of Hell Burger, I let loose on the building with a great deal of relief. Shaking dry, I saw the light from inside the club glow across the sidewalk in front of it. Running in a crouch, zipping up, I made for the Reliant.

About five guys, each the size of Godzilla, staggered across the parking lot not giving much of a damn about the noise they made. Luckily, the Reliant was made before they put those automatic headlights on cars that came on anytime the engine was started. I didn't want the headlights on until they were well ahead of me. The traffic was sparse now, most people were home watching *Law and Order* reruns and commercials to enhance your life with a miracle of modern living.

In no particular hurry, I followed their Subaru north along London Road, skirting the blackness of Lake Superior. My first thought was that they were headed to the town of Two Harbors, twenty-seven miles north of Duluth. Instead, just as the Duluth proper ended and Highway 61 took over, they turned off onto the scenic Brighton Beach Road. The area we were headed led to a very elite neighborhood that enjoyed privacy overlooking the mighty lake. Swank homes ranging from a half-million to even higher ridiculously over riced levels, graced the shoreline. The Subaru taillights were tiny in the distance I was leaving between us, but unmistakable. Then, they got bright as the brakes were applied, and turned into a driveway. I got a little closer and pulled over, turning my lights off. I knew where they pulled in and wanted to make sure they couldn't see me on the road.

It might be too soon, but I got impatient, and moved ahead. I slowed at the driveway, noted the address on the mailbox, and kept moving. I made a U-turn about a mile further, and went back. Passing the driveway again, there was nothing but blackness and more nothing. My inclination was to dismount and go snooping, but two elements took over, stopping me. It was too dark, and I was too scared.

When I got to the main road leading back into Duluth, it occurred to me that I was passing the old water plant where Rikki and I saw the stiff that had been executed. Coincidence? I don't think so. Too close to the suspicions on Brighton Beach Road.

There was no way I was going home now, so I tooled up to the Miller Hill area where the Pink Power investigators operated from. I had a key, but as I was about to unlock the door, it occurred to me that I didn't know if the place had an alarm. The last thing I wanted to deal with was a rent-a-cop from some security agency. And, I was even less inclined to explain my entry to a real cop. So, I camped out in front of the place. I had to sneak around to the back a few times to take a leak, and I was craving a good belt of the Jack Daniels that Brew had stolen from me. Brew! I still didn't know how much trust I should place in her.

I knew it was daytime because, oddly enough, it was light outside. Duh. And, I was awoke by Jeanine rapping on the window, holding a peace offering in a Starbucks cup. God, I loved that girl.

She led me inside and sure enough, she keyed in the password to the alarm system. See, I wasn't nearly as dumb as everyone thought. I was way too old to be spending the night in my car and my bones, joints, and muscles were having a serious argument with each other, each one trying to out-hurt the other.

I stretched out in Jeanine's genuine leather meant-for-guests-only easy chair, thinking I could sleep there every night. Her soft melodious voice barked at me,

"What the hell are you doing here? You have a home. Such as it is. Try sleeping there. The neighbors are already spooky of us."

"Spooky of us? I don't think that's a real sentence."

"Shut up."

"Okay." I let a few moments go by to give her a chance to ingest more coffee. "Wanna know what I did?"

Her sarcasm was not appreciated. "Raped an old lady?"

"No. She ran too fast." I put on my serious face and told her, "I think I know where the dock workers are. Or at least where some of them hang out."

She stared at me for a long time before throwing her hands up, "So where? Are you going to keep it a secret? Tell me."

I had some fatherly and sage advice to offer, "Jeanine, is there ever a time that you are not in your you-know-what cycle?"

"Fuck you. Then don't tell me." She gave herself a moment to pout, then relented, "Okay, you saw something. Please, tell Mama what it was and I'll give you a cookie."

"All right, as long as you're forcing me. On Brighton Beach Road." I gave her the number and took a moment to sip more life-saving juice from Starbucks.

She set her cup down and started opening file drawers, mumbling, "Oh, shit, no. I don't believe it." She laid a manila folder on her desk and sat in front of it. "On second thought, maybe I do believe it."

"Jeanine, you're talking in code. Share with me."

She held up the folder, spouting, "That's the address for Burton and Gloria Fields. He's the owner of Great Lakes Shipping." She looked up and we both said in unison, "That's where Rikki is." Finally, we agreed on something.

Back in the "good old days" when this place was just, Norby Klein, Detective, I would have poured a shot of Old Mr. Boston into my Starbucks cup right now. It always had an effect on my sensory vision helping me think and put things in order. I wasn't allowed to do that anymore, so I had to use my natural cunning ability to guide me. Which meant, I was clueless. We had to get into the Fields house. Jeanine then came up with a brilliant idea.

"We have to get into the Fields house."

Gee why didn't I think of that? "Okay, Sherlock, give us a plan."

She smiled, and by some form of magic, she proposed a plan. "I'll walk up and ring the doorbell."

Over my objections, she persisted, and after explaining to me, she really had a plan. Not a great one, but it was something that only she could pull off.

Jeanine was one of those women who can perform on any stage. She could come off equally well as a society snob or a drunk hooker. She was adaptable to any situation because she was fearless. Dressed smartly in an outfit from Nordstrom's, that she intended to return later, she drove her 1966 red Fiat Dino boldly up the driveway to the Fields estate. We had our cell phones on so I could hear most of what was going on with her. I waited well down the road, hopefully, out of sight.

I could almost hear her stiletto heels clicking on the concrete driveway as she approached the front door. Places like this did not have doorbells. They announce visitors with chimes offering renditions of old Italian operas. The Fields were evidently adventurous, because their particular door chime rang out "Fur Elise," which I believed was German. Those rascals.

From my end, the voices at the door were muffled, but for Jeanine, she responded to a very large man wearing a dirty tee shirt and jeans. Duluth upper society must be changing. His voice was as hairy and dirty as he was, "Yeah?"

"Hi, there, I'm Jeanine Forrester. I'd like to see Gloria please." Her smile had charm and appeal written all across her face.

His response was as dull as his wit, "Huh?"

"I'm Gloria's Avon lady. She knows I'm coming. Would you get her please." She held up a tiny paper bag emblazoned with the Avon logo to prove her story.

Gort the Horrible just didn't get it, but the scene was saved by a being of higher intelligence stepping in. "Stans, I'll take this." Looking at the ravishing fresh face standing at the door, the new guy became more interested than the Neanderthal. "Hello, can I help you?"

With a fresh approach, Jeanine laid it out again, "Yes, I have an appointment with Gloria. She ordered some Avon, and I need to see her."

He stretched his hand out. "I'll see that she gets it."

"That's fine, but I have a new blush that would be fabulous for her, and I need to collect $14.95." Her charm would have altered the course of history if she could have used that bit on Genghis Khan.

Unknown to him, the guy at the door just became Jeanine's victim. "Uh, all right, come on in. I'll get her. But you have to wait here."

"That's fine." She slid into the entryway, taking in all sights and sound she could capture. About ten minutes later, Gloria Fields came crawling out of wherever she was being kept.

Startled, she did a double take. "Jeanine, what?"

Act two, scene one. Jeanine took over. "Hi, Gloria. I have the Avon you ordered and an absolutely marvelous blush for you to try."

It took a moment, but Mrs. Fields stepped into the play. "Oh, fine. Thank you." She was unsure of what step to take next, so gave the lead to Jeanine.

"The light in here is just not right. Lets step outside for a moment."

Mrs. Fields looked around as if to ask permission, and then saw the sinister man standing in the living room, watching. Quietly, she said, "I don't know if I should. I'm being watched."

Pasting on her smile, Jeanine said, loud enough, "Just step into the daylight. Right outside." Before anybody could digest what was happening, Jeanine had Mrs. Fields out the door. Quickly, she asked, "Do you want to get out of here? Now?"

"I, I don't dare. My husband is still in there and he won't be safe."

"Fine, I won't force you, but tell me. Is there a young blonde woman in there?"

Hesitant, Gloria finally sputtered, "Yes, Rikki is her name. Do you know her?"

"Is she okay?"

"Yes, she's one of them. She's nice but very secretive. I try to talk to her, but, I don't know. She's different. Not like them. What's happening? We're in trouble and we don't know what to do."

"How about a tall woman. Blonde. Kathleen. Is she there?"

"She was, but only once. They keep talking about her. She's the scariest of all of them. Oh, this is so horrible."

Jeanine handed her the Avon prop, and told her, "Have faith. We're going to help you. If you can, tell Rikki to call Norby. Got that?"

The nervous lady nodded, "Yes, but . . ."

"Just stay out of their way and do what they say. You at least know we're aware of what's happening."

Jeanine watched the old lady go back inside, then climbed into her Fiat, and left. In a hurry.

CHAPTER
FIFTEEN

● ●

I TRIED FOLLOWING THE FIAT BACK TO THE OFFICE, but she was light years ahead of me. Damn, just once, it would be so nice to step on the gas and get a response from the car. Then, the chirping started and my mind processed a dozen things that would make a chirping noise before my Reliant quit running. However, I doubted that my car chirping would make my pocket vibrate. My phone was ringing. I hastily put aside the notion of keeping the vibrating phone in my shorts.

Years ago, when life was simple, telephones were black objects that sat on desks, and had normal rings. If you weren't near a phone, you didn't talk. Now, I fumbled with the tiny vibrating piece-of-crap phone, thinking that if I ignored it, the world would end. A phone was ringing, or buzzing, or screaming, or bonging, or doing any one of a million sets of obnoxious noises, and I was veering all over the road trying to say, "Hello?"

I finally got it to my ear and yelled, "What?"

"Dad?" The tiny voice on the other end our electronic connection was like an angel singing. Salvation with a real person who was alive and not dead or missing. "Dad? It's me Rikki. Can you talk?"

Dad? Oh oh. "Hi, Rikki. Yeah, it's me, Dad. How are you, honey?" I fought with the momentum of the car and wrestled it across two lanes of pissed off drivers, landing on the sidewalk, one inch from a phone pole.

"I haven't talked to you for a while, Dad. How's it going?"

"Going great, sweetie. What are you up to?"

"Just hanging with some friends. I miss you, Dad. Can we get together?"

There it was. The connection. "Sure, babe. When and where?"

"Lets meet at the Leif Erickson Park Rose Garden, tomorrow around ten in the morning. Okay? Just like we used to do. I want to catch up on all the news."

"Tomorrow. Just like we used to do."

"Bye, Dad. Love you."

The tiny electronic gizmo went dead, and so did I. I had to get with Jeanine, fast. Rikki's call so soon after she left the Fields place had to have a connection. Bingo.

I managed to get back onto London Road without killing anyone, and made it all the way to the office. The Fiat and Brew's muscle truck were parked in front, which relegated me to a graveled spot in back by the garbage can. Luckily, the can was a different color than my Reliant.

We decided to have Brew rent an inconspicuous car and tail Rikki as she left the Fields' place. It was anybody's guess what she would be driving, or if she would be alone. Jeanine would be at the gardens well before the 10:00 a.m. time Rikki mentioned. There was a reason she picked that particular place, and I needed to talk to her dad to see what was significant about it. The three of us would be connected by radios, and I'd wear an ear plug.

Sy needed to know what his daughter was doing and that she was safe. I was not too convinced on the safe part, but, we'd see. Also, I just like talking to the guy.

Sy Thielges kept his house in pretty good order. Not a neat fanatic, but he had learned to at least pick up after himself, and keep the dirty dishes in the kitchen. I could learn a lot from him, but that's a tall order I don't want to follow.

Sitting at the old kitchen table, we nursed the familiar Grain Belt NordEast. The faded red-and-white oil cloth had been protecting the chipped painted surface of the table for over twenty years, and I found it rather comfortable. We played with the labels on the sweaty bottles, demonstrating our manhood by pinching the bottle caps into a taco shape. Guy stuff. The wet rings on the oil cloth were played with as well.

I told him as much as I could, or dared, and asked what was special about the Leif Erickson Park. His smile told me more than his words could. "We used to go there when she was just a tyke. She took her first steps there. Until she was old enough to understand the truth, I told her that her mother's spirit was dancing among the flowers. We never went to a church much, but on most Sunday mornings we'd sit on a particular bench and think that being there was as good as a church. She'd help me pack a lunch and we'd pretend we were the only people on earth and it was our special place. I'd read her the story, *Heidi*, and she'd pretend to be her, and I'd be her grandfather, Alp-Ohi, only nicer. It was our get-away place where she felt safe."

I stopped him there, not wanting to invade their private place. I was buzzed on NordEast so I let the Reliant take me home.

Early the next morning we met at the Pink Power office and checked out the communication. Brew had borrowed a light-blue Chevy Cavalier, which would blend in real easy. Jeanine's Fiat was too much of an attention getter, so she hauled her father's old 1962 Buick Skylark out of storage. He had willed it to her, and she didn't have the heart to get rid of it. For stake-outs, it was perfect and nondescript. My Reliant was trashy enough to be suited for any occasion.

Jeanine left first, which meant that I was alone with Brew. It was uncomfortable, until she straightened out a kink in our relationship. "So, dick head, are we good in what we got together?"

"Oh, Brew, you have such a way with words. I hope we're okay. Are we?"

"Don't get melancholy, man. We fucked, that's all. You got to sample the candy, and I got to be happy with a middle-aged guy with a beer gut. What's not to like?"

I tried to think of a follow up, but there was no way I'd come up with anything that would cement our friendship any better. She did that for me. "Don't try so hard to like me, Norby. Not many people do. I scare most of them. We'll work together, and I won't burn you. What's important is, do you trust me?"

I had to be honest. "I'm trying, Brew. I want to and I can't find any reason not to trust you. It'll fall into place. We'll be good together."

"Cool, man." She high-fived me and almost knocked me over. I watched her leave in the Cavalier, and I left for my part of the game.

The Leif Erickson Park Rose Garden was an oddity that not too many people were aware of. Besides being one of the midwest's few formal English-style rose gardens, the park was architecturally significant for being constructed over Duluth's I-35 expressway. As you strolled around the park, little did you know that below your feet, trucks and cars were playing tag in a civilized demo-derby. The place included over 3,000 rose bushes representing more than 100 varieties, among its flowering landscape plantings. That's as much as I knew about flowers, and if Sy hadn't told me, I'd be even more stupid. I found the bench he had mentioned and sat down with the lunch Jeanine had put together. She didn't trust me, as my favorite was peanut butter and Miracle Whip. Add a cold beer, and it became a gourmet dinner. I peeked under the cover and hoped those weren't egg salad. She tossed in a couple cans of Pepsi and some potato chips that were getting smashed by my handling technique.

The microphones were picking up better than we had planned. Brew was a little fuzzy, being too far away. As her tail got closer, she came in clearer. My leg was vibrating in a nervous dance, and I realized I was scared. I wasn't absolutely certain where Jeanine was planted, but I knew she'd never be spotted. All three of us were armed.

Brew came on. "They're a block ahead of me, pulling into the parking lot. I'm hanging back. If you start yelling, I'm coming in."

"Jeanine? You got sight of me?"

"Yes, you bone-head. I'm right behind you. Shut up and pay attention."

"Yes, dear."

CHAPTER
SIXTEEN

● ●

I DIDN'T SEE RIKKI AT FIRST, BUT I COULD FEEL her presence. I started shaking and bit my lip to make the pain put me back into a work mode. Man, that hurt. As expected, she made her appearance from the right. I turned to look and almost crapped in my pants. She was different. Changed. She walked slowly, almost sadly. My feet were too heavy, so I stayed anchored at the park bench, waiting. She got to me and threw her arms around me hugging long and tight. I wanted to cry.

She wasn't alone. A tall man, built like a 1957 Buick Road Master, was standing on the path about ten yards from us. He had his arms crossed, and if I knew anything, I knew he was packing. He wore a leather coat and had a close-shaved head that topped off a look that said "I'm mean." I looked hard at him but Rikki pulled me away. "That's Gordo. I think he's Russian, or Greek. Not sure. He's my body guard, and to make sure I go back with him. He doesn't speak much, and I don't understand much of what he does say. Let's walk."

She threaded her arm through mine and we slowly strode through the garden, Gordo always behind. Maybe Jeanine would shoot him.

She spoke softly so our shadow wouldn't overhear. "When Jeanine came to the Fields house and gave her the message, it was a perfect time to make contact. I had to stay under wraps long enough for them to trust me. I used the call my Dad idea, and they bought it."

"Rikki, you look like crap. What are they doing to you? You have to get out."

"No. Too soon. I'm getting an idea of what they are doing and it has to stop. We can meet from time to time, and I'll fill you in on what I know."

"You didn't answer me. What're they doing to you? You look ten years older."

She stopped walking, then started up again. This was a sore spot for her. "I'm okay. Don't worry about me. Don't ask so many questions, so I can get out what I've got to tell you. I can't waste a lot of time."

I pulled her closer.

"Norby, they think you're my dad. Go along with it. For starters, don't trust anyone. There's some outside influence that's telling them what to do and what to watch for. The Fields are prisoners and Burton's brother, Gordon, is calling the shots. Their business is shipping things out from the Duluth Harbor. I'm being given more freedom and can wander around listening. I'll call you in about a week. We can meet someplace else."

"I'm worried about you, Rikki. I think you're in too deep."

"Leave me alone, Dad. I know what I'm doing. I saw you brought a lunch. You must have talked to Sy. Thanks, but there's no time for it now. I have to go and you can't take the risk of following me. A blue car tailed us here and that has to stop. It's too dangerous. I'll be at the Fields place as far as I know. Give Sy my regards."

We had strolled back to the bench where she separated herself from me. On tip toe, she rose up and kissed me, soft, sweet, and quick. "Bye, Dad. Tell Brian I still have the green M&M. I miss him. Oh, and don't forget my cat."

There was a sad finality to her voice, an acceptance of a fate she had no control over. Like a hovering vulture Gordo swept her away, and she was gone. Someday, I was going to kill Gordo.

CHAPTER
SEVENTEEN

● ●

ALWAYS A STEP AHEAD OF ME, Jeanine had recorded my conversation with Rikki. We tooled back to the Pink Power office to analyze what was recorded. It became apparent that there was, or were, outside sources that we needed to be careful of. Jeanine, the most resourceful of us, "Who else can be involved but the cops?"

Brew added, "List them. That dope Snerd, the chief, the mayor, Grosslein, even that fed guy."

From what I knew, "The phone we took from the surveillance van apparently didn't belong to anyone. There were no other calls, in or out, on the Sim card. What's the name of the guy you kicked the shit out of in the van?"

Jeanine opened a manila folder, scanning a list. "Desmond. Clark Desmond. He works with the feds."

Brew and I had the same idea, but she was quicker, naturally. "Do we trust Tellworth? Can we ask if there might be a spook in the loop?"

I knew enough to answer, "No. We can't trust anyone. Whoever called Desmond knew he would do as told. That means that the surveillance in the van was just a prop, and Rikki was set up to be taken. She's bait. She's going to be allowed to give us as much information as they want us to know."

Brew, finally confused, "Why? For what purpose? They have to know we're looking at what they're doing."

I tried to be logical, "Pay attention. They don't care if we know anything. They're so implanted on the docks they think they have carte-blanche to run anyway they want. They have protection from someone very high up."

Brew was paying attention. "Who's higher than the mayor?"

Jeanine stood up and started pacing. I've seen this before and I just let her put the pieces together. She turned to lay her logic on us. "What was the ambassador involved in? International stuff, right? Hell, he had millions from some Arab potentate to buy weapons for international trade. When he got killed, and the money disappeared, whoever we're dealing with couldn't just walk away. This business was already in force then. I doubt if they are crippled by loosing those goddamn bonds, but they, or should I say, she, isn't going to leave it alone. For now, I'd leave the mayor on the list, but look higher up. There has to be a government connection to be on this much of an operation."

Jeanine looked at me, "Kathleen Pierpont wants your ass more than the bonds, Norby. You have to get away, or you're going to be traveling to some foreign port as refuse in one of those containers."

Hmm, not my idea of a vacation. I knew what I had to do and wasn't sure it was the smartest move. So what's new? I stood up. "I've got something to do. I'll let you know when Rikki calls again. She has to know her cover is a sham and get out. I'll disappear if I can take her with me."

Jeanine had an idea of what was going to happen, or she'd never sit still and watch it take place. I just hoped she knew enough to keep it to herself.

I placed the phone call and arranged for the meeting to take place in the Union Cemetery, where Laura was buried. I visit the site once in a while wishing things were different. I imagined Laura would agree. She died a horrible death at the hands of despicable monster I was going to kill, someday. The secret that Laura and I shared was the location of the capricious bonds that everyone was looking for. That was a detail I'd take to my grave like she did. "Yeah, we fooled them, honey. You and me."

I saw the beam of the flashlight bobbing to guide my pissed off visitor to my location. I stepped back into the darkness watching, not the beam from the flashlight, but the space behind it.

FBI agent, Frank Tellworth, stood at the spot by Laura's headstone, looking for me. Hoarsely rasping out my name, trying to get me out of hiding, he threw in a few expletives to let me know he was upset. When he finally yelled at me to have sex with myself, he turned to stomp off.

While he was busy with verbal assaults on my character, I circled back to his car. By then I was assured he was alone. As he stepped to the driver's door, I presented myself. "Hi, Frank. Come here often?"

He jumped and the flashlight flew out of his hand, dismantling on the pavement. Good. Now I wouldn't have to argue with him to turn the damn thing off.

"Jesus, Klein, don't do that." I gave him a moment to catch his breath, and he lashed out, "What the fuck are you pulling? Are you crazy? I could arrest you for, for . . ."

"For what, Frank? Scaring you? Come on, let's talk a walk and talk about something."

"Fuck you, Klein, we'll talk in my car."

"Then go home without talking, Frank. If you do I'll know I'm right about the stink attached to you." I knew that would grab him, so he stepped closer. "This way. I want to be sure you aren't bugged." I slid behind him and ran my hands over the front and back of his shirt. Smooth; no bug on him.

"All right, Klein, I'm all ears, and if you don't explain this I'll have your ass in an unpleasant place. What's up? You know this clandestine bullshit doesn't take place in a modern world anymore."

I leveled with him, paying close attention to his response. "You've got a traitor in your office."

His eyes glowed in the darkness, and he hissed, "Tell me more."

"Are you aware that Officer Loretta Thielges was set up to be abducted by the crew of dock hands you said were being investigated?"

He leaned closer. "Keep talking."

"The night she disappeared from the Conestoga Club your surveillance van was supposed to be monitoring her contacts with the big guys. We checked the van, and all we found was your agent, Clark Desmond, with his dick in an under-age girl. He got a phone call from an unknown caller telling him to abort the operation. The call came from an untraceable source.

"I've met with Officer Thielges since, and she has the idea that she's infiltrating the mob, thinking she's going to feed us information. We got into the house they've commandeered and discovered she's being used as bait. If you're involved it won't take long for the telltale sign to surface. If it does, I'll kill you. Understand?"

He whispered, "Oh, shit. No, I don't know about any of this."

Now that pissed me off. "And why don't you, Frank? Why am I, a destitute, washed up PI able to find out about this, when the FBI can't?"

He paced a bit, then said, "We have another plant in the ring. You can threaten me all you want, but I'll never reveal who it is. Yes, I know Thielges is there, and that was planned to keep attention from our guy."

"Is she in trouble, Frank?"

"Not as far as I know."

"Get her out."

His hesitation told me all I needed to know. Then he confirmed my suspicion, "No. Thielges stays where she is. We're getting close, and the more innocent Thielges is, the closer we can get."

I didn't like what I was hearing, getting hotter by the moment. Time to become the asshole he thought I was. I leaned into him, quiet but with conviction, "Frank, read my lips. If she's hurt, you die." I could feel him seething as I turned and disappeared into the blackness.

CHAPTER
EIGHTEEN

• •

RIKKI CALLED ME FOUR DAYS LATER. Her demeanor was not nearly as bubbly as before, sounding drawn and weary. "Hi, Dad, how ya doing?"

I choked on the words, trying to sound upbeat, but there was no up. "Hi, honey. I miss you. Any chance we can go fishing? In the boat?"

Her answer came back slow, "I don't think I'd have that much time. How about a walk along the beach on the Park Point peninsula? Remember how I loved to walk on the sand with . . ." She cut her melancholy comment short, and quickly told me, "I gotta go, Dad. Tomorrow, ten in the morning. I'll meet you at our favorite spot. Love you."

Favorite spot. The phone was dead and so was I.

The most difficult part of the day, after the depressing call from Rikki, was convincing her father, Sy, that all was well and his baby was doing a fantastic job. Trying to keep the conversation casual, and prodding him for information without setting off any alarms, I finally got him to mention how, as a little girl, she loved to run along the sandy shoreline at the Park Point Recreation Area. Bypassing the NordEast routine, we shared a few cups of coffee. I saw he was happy enough to avoid it as well. Too much mind stuff in the way. I should really stop drinking both since they go straight to my bladder.

The next day, Jeanine and some bozo she picked up one day, sat in a rented deck-boat off the shore. A couple of fishing poles stuck out from the boat with Jeanine and her indentured slave making a show of casting and staring at bobbers. If they actually caught something, it would be an old shoe, or a tire. The day was gray and dismal, a slight breeze wafting across the sand. A little stronger off-shore, it kept the anchor rope taught.

I wore a nylon wind breaker hanging long enough to cover the hardware stuck into the back of my pants. Damn glad to have the wind protection. I had a purpose for being there, so there was no reason to make a show of being busy at something.

Brew was staying hidden in the cabin of the boat. For my own reason, I didn't want her involved, but she was needed. I didn't object to Jeanine's boy-toy, and didn't want to make an issue over Brew. See, I wasn't always stupid.

The giantess had some training someplace seeming to fit in whenever plain old sleuthing wasn't enough. She had a bag of tricks that must have come from whatever her CIA background gave her. Her revealing that she had a stint at undercover in the CIA was just a teaser to impress us. It did, but I don't like unknown factors. Mysteries. Cloudy stuff. Today, though, she was a positive addition to the fishing trip. I could imagine her throwing the boy-toy overboard when this was over.

Brew hid her sculptured torso in the cabin of the boat working the Biodish-1000 bionic ear. Designed for long distance stake-outs, it would amplify sounds while the built-in monocular would allow watching and recording everything, all from a safe distance. She controlled the Revo Professional 650 TVL CCD Surveillance Camera like a pro, which I had no doubt she was. The term "pro" was an ambiguous term to cover too many things. More unknowns. Her past went deeper than that, and someday, I was going to find out just why she was here with us. Agent Tellworth's revelation that Rikki was not the only plant in the mob just became more interesting.

Show time. The Subaru I had followed earlier to the Fields estate snaked its way along Minnesota Avenue, in no apparent hurry, coming to a halt thirty yards in front of me. I think I made Gordo as the driver, and there was another dude next to him. The back door opened and Rikki stepped out, staring at me. I started walking toward her, but she put her hand up, and I stopped.

I assumed a stance with my hands behind my back, one hand on the butt of my Sig Sauer Model P226 - 9mil semi-auto pistol. I had loaded the magazine with an armor piercing round in every other spot. If I needed to stop a man or a vehicle, I had no doubt I could do it.

She slowly stepped in my direction, leaving the door ajar. "C'mon, walk along the shore with me." He voice was hard, and sad. She threaded her arm in mine pulling me to where she wanted to go. Her head rested on my shoulder, and I felt the sadness and tension immediately.

"Rikki, you have to get out, now. I think they know you're a plant. There's another . . ."

That was all I got out. "Shut up and listen to me. I know all about that, but they still want me around. Entertainment factor. The ships they load with containers—twenty-foot-high cube dry. They're loaded with human cargo kidnapped from Mexico, Guatemala, Cambodia, and Vietnam. The prize is the American girls, but they never live long enough to get this far. Maybe a few runaways, I dunno."

This last fact stunned me and brought the whole Marci Hudson story raging through my head. That was the case that sent me to hell. Marci Hudson's daughter was kidnapped and forced into white slavery in Mexico. After that, I wound up here.

Rikki knew I had sent my brain in a different direction, tugging my arm to wake me up. "Pay attention, Dad. I only have a couple minutes here."

She went on, "The harbor master here gets the cargo loaded on board passing inspection. Name of Duane Marglott, I think. Two tee's. They took my car. Trust me, I'll get out when I can, but not now. There's a spy in the police department that tells them everything. They're way ahead of the game. You have to find who it is and get rid of them."

She walked me back to the Subaru, turned into me and said, "Kiss me, Dad. Don't worry. I'm doing what I want to do." She stretched on her tip toes, kissed me, and left to disappear into the Subaru. Before she turned away, I spotted a small drop in the corner of her eye. The last thing she said, "Take care of my cat."

I hated cats.

The Subaru slowly backed up, turned around, and left in no particular hurry. They were confident enough to enjoy what they thought was a free ticket for whatever they wanted. They had protection.

The mic planted in my ear screamed at me, "Norby, look out, behind you."

I spun around, the Sig at the end of my arm with way too much pressure on the trigger. Sy Thielges came tumbling out of the bushes with a twelve-gauge shotgun clutched in his ham sized fist. I screamed at him, "Sy, goddamit, put that blunderbuss down. Now."

Staring at the empty space left by the Subaru which took his daughter away, the man wasn't concerned about me and my tirade. But he did know what he was supposed to do next. He jacked the slide back, caught the ejected shell in mid-air, and locked the chamber open.

Looking down the road where the Subaru wasn't anymore, he muttered, "She looks like shit, Norby." He looked through the mist in his eyes and told me, "I'll never see her again, will I."

He gave up the old Browning shotgun and slumped on his huge frame, beaten.

The mic screamed in my ear again, tearing out any form of hearing I had left. I tugged on it to get the damn thing out of my head, while listening to Brew call me a few names and tell me they were returning the boat. I suspected that Jeanine's boy-toy had to get home or get grounded by his mom.

I followed Sy's 1979 F150 back to his place and proceeded to help him get incredibly drunk. When Jagermeister and Old Mister Boston brandy were combined with careless abandon on quantity, it became lethal. If anyone was ever curious as to why the toilet and sink were so close together, it was so drunks who go unchecked through an idiot stage can barf and get the shits at the same time. This was where the phrase, "I'll never drink again," was born.

I didn't remember falling into the bath tub, but that's where I woke up eight hours later. I had laid in a crumpled position so long I was certain I had contracted polio overnight. I tried screaming for help, but forgot who I would be calling to, and what I should elucidate in doing so. Through a painful rolling motion I managed to finally find the floor with my feet. It was there I discovered that not all of my expelled waste had hit the intended disposal sites.

I must have come in with shoes, but I wasn't certain. With the help from the wall and door frame I was able to get myself, such as I was, into the kitchen. I looked at the face Sy was wearing and couldn't imagine how he managed to piss on it. I'm sure I didn't do it.

Working together we put together enough hash browns, onions, Tabasco sauce, sausage, eggs, and coffee, to force real blood to flow happily through our hardening arteries.

I gave his Browning back to him and went home for a wash and rinse cycle. I fell asleep in the shower, waking up to the freezing cold spray, hunched over in the tub. Much to my disgust, apparently, I wasn't done expelling waste.

CHAPTER
NINETEEN

● ●

A FEW MORE HOURS OF SLEEP GAVE ME ENOUGH fortitude to locate another pair of shoes. They were both the same color. Cool for me. I needed help, badly, and crawled to Mrs. Feldstein's door. If science were to discover her chicken soup, the race to find a cure for cancer, and the mystery of stem cell healing would be over. My feeble knock caught her attention. Her muted warning from behind the multiple locked door challenged any intruder. "I got a gun in here, so just get gone. Go. Now. I gonna shoot."

I rasped, "Mrs. Feldstein, it's me, Norby." Like magic, I listened to the chains being loosened, the moat being drained, and like the gates to heaven, the door swung open revealing her massive muumuu-covered frame. She wrapped her arms around me, "Oh, my little tinok, you come to Mama." If the hangover didn't kill me, I'd smother in her ample bosom. But, I loved her.

Mrs. Feldstein lived in the luxury of her deceased husband's social security check, food stamps, and rent credit. At the end of the Pierpont missing bond case, along with several charities, and Mrs. Feldstein, mysterious amounts of money began flowing into their coffers. Some unknown do-gooder, I suppose.

Mrs. Feldstein was my guardian angel, having warned me about unwanted intruders more than once. The numbers tattooed on her arm gave her a status not matched by many others. A poster child for Spoolies, they were growing from her head like mushrooms. Her one luxury was a weekly visit to the beauty shop where she could be pampered and share in meaningless gossip.

I now sat at her kitchen table letting her fawn over me, spooning that marvelous greasy chicken liquid into my face. She made me undress to wash and iron my clothes, and it was then I discovered my skivvies were on backwards. I'm not crazy about matzo balls, but she insisted they would stick to my ribs, once they got past my teeth.

A new Norby Klein, I stepped out onto Superior Avenue and was accosted by sunlight. Quick, get away before I disintegrate. My stumbling took me to my favorite place in the world, Hell Burger. Angie's stain in the pavement was slowly fading, and I walked around it, not wishing to desecrate her last earthly presence. Even for a waste like Angie, what happened to her was a tragedy. Nobody deserved that. Well, maybe a few did, but not her.

Inside, I adjusted to the darkness and greeted Pappy, propped up behind the bar. He was nursing a cup of coffee, reading the *Duluth News Tribune* Sports section. The exiting news of the Duluth High School Wild Cats getting new uniforms was keeping him deeply engrossed enough to ignore me. I stepped behind the bar and poured myself a cup of rich-smelling coffee. A bump of bourbon topped it off just fine. So, in the aftermath of my marathon with Sy, I vowed to never drink again. Shut up.

I took a seat at the end of the bar which I had designated as my office. "Morning, Pappy."

He slurred back, "Fuck you."

"Good coffee, Pappy."

"It'll cost you a buck."

"No doughnuts today?"

"Princess Kate and what's his name were in earlier and scarfed them all down."

I glanced to my left and there weren't any sticky note messages on the wall, and I grew tired of listening to Pappy tell me how wonderful I was, so I decided to quit being a dick head and go to Stu's barbeque. If I got drunk again I'd have an excuse to not show up, but Noreen made the best potato salad in Duluth. Stu was pretty good on burning hamburger, which made the invitation more enticing. Also, I was curious on how the pudgy daughter, Isabelle, was doing and what plan she was hatching to get noticed.

The Grosslein family lived in a congested neighborhood overlooking the Duluth proper. A respectable area that grew in the sixties when a contractor put up a hundred homes designed for the just-starting-out crowd. Originally selling for ten grand, inflation had increased the value to eight times that amount. Unfortunately, the natural order of decay and more modern construction in the suburbs made the homes an albatross. You were in now and would never get out.

I had to park a block away. I wasn't aware of the Grosslein's being so popular. I considered turning around but the street was too congested, and by the time I neared the corner I found a spot. Damn. Approaching the house I stopped and stared at the graffiti someone had stuck into Stu's crabgrass. A large blue and white billboard emblazoned with Stu Grosslein For City Council. You're Man Of Action across the front. Jeez. In the process of turning back to my car, I was approached by a beautiful young lady who I would consider taking with me. Until I recognized her. Shocked, I yelped, "Isabelle?"

She had long brunette hair draping over shapely breasts discretely covered by a brown chiffon dress. The legs holding this assembly up were sculpted into curvaceous champagne goblet stems. "Isabelle?"

She stepped boldly to me and put her arms around my neck. "Hi, Mr. Klein. Daddy said you'd be here. I'm so glad." Then she kissed me.

Embarrassed, I pushed her back and adroitly asked, "Isabelle?"

She smiled and did a pirouette to allow me the pleasure of her panoramic self. "You like?" I wasn't allowed a response as she took hold of my arm to lead me through the crowd. She handed me a campaign brochure, then asked, "You aren't going to throw up again are you? Mommy would be devastated. I think the stain from last time is still in the carpet, but she keeps a throw rug over it. Let's go see Daddy."

Before she could foist me off on Daddy, I had to know. I stopped her forward motion, and asked, "Isabelle, stop. Before I go another step you're going to tell me what you did with the old Isabelle."

That smile again. "You approve then?"

"Of course."

"Well, I owe it all to you."

"Bullshit, Isabelle. I could never be responsible for being involved in any part of getting you to look so . . . so . . . beautiful."

Another smile. I really felt awkward.

Clutching my arm again, she explained, "Remember when you had a talk with me about shocking parents, and finding values, and self respect? I really thought about it and went on a crash course with destiny. As I started changing, so did my perspective on respect. For myself and how others see me."

I pulled her close and kissed the top of her sweet-smelling head. "Congratulations, Isabelle. You're gorgeous."

Then I found my own ground when she said, "Besides, Daddy said if I didn't make a change, I'd turn out just like you." She beamed, "Wouldn't that be awful? Daddy's at the grill. I have to meet some people. See ya." I watched her prance away and stuck the vote-for-Stu brochure in a planter. People were milling about holding paper plates and balancing plastic beer cups. Aha, a kegger. I bypassed the front door and worked my way to the backyard. The smoke billowing up had to be where Stu was, so I pushed through a larger crowd to the keg. I downed one cup, then filled it again for my socializing tool.

I leaned against the grill, unaware that it was hot. Duh. Quickly recovering and dousing the smoldering patch on my shirt, I said, "Hi, Stu."

I knew he had been drinking all day because he was happy to see me. Waving his spatula, he threw his arms around me, "Norby, glad to see you, old buddy. Got a beer? Good. How about a burger? You need anything?"

"I'm fine, Stu. I just met Isabelle. She's looking great."

He gave me a confusing look that only a father of a sixteen-year-old girl could wear. "Yeah, she's doing good now. Grades are up and she's popular. Lots of boys, Norby. Lots of boys hanging around. Want a beer?"

I held my cup aloft, "I'm fine, Stu. Going into politics, huh?"

"Yeah, thought Id try expanding myself and see if I can't do some good for the city. I got your vote, don't I?"

I slapped his back and felt the layer of excess flesh jiggle. "Hell, yes, councilman, you got my vote." Wandering away, I added, out of his earshot, "Yeah, you and Elmer Fudd."

Stu, in spite of his inebriated state, burned a good burger. Enough garbage heaped on it, and it was palatable. Good beer, too. The crowd was a decent size, considering that only four people here really knew Stu Grosslein. The other three were Don Ness, the mayor himself, Chief of Police Gordon Ramsay, and none other than good old Darrel Snerd. Darrel and I gave each other the finger and stayed away to avoid a conflict.

I wandered into the kitchen to see what I could scrounge from Mrs. Grosslein that didn't have charcoal attached to it. I spied her plump little body, adorned with a white apron, shuffling among the crowd with a tray of little artsy-fartsy cracker things. She had a nervous edge to her, and the sweat dripping from her forehead was totally not her. Usually calm and level, this was a new twist.

I moved to her, "Hi, Noreen. You look overwhelmed."

Balancing the tray, she put her hand on my shoulder, "Oh, Norby. A friendly face for once. I'm so glad you came."

Speaking loud over the din of voices, "What the hell is going on, Noreen? All this for a piss-ant seat on the City Council?"

She shrugged, "Stu thinks it'll give him prestige for better openings on the force. What do you think?"

I took the tray from her and handed it to a tall woman who looked like a buzzard, her beak sticking out searching for dead meat. "Here, could you take care of this? Thanks." I guided Noreen out of the kitchen and downstairs to the family room. There were a few couples talking politics, and the lovely Isabelle was sucking face with a pimple farm. I pulled him off. "Isabelle, can you get these people out of here and bring us your Dad's bottle of Canadian Club? Please."

Two minutes later, the new sex symbol returned with the quart and two plastic cups. Her smile and giggle had a message attached to it that said something about her being able to do it if we could. "Thanks, Isabelle. Why don't you go take charge of crowd control or something." She bounded off giggling. Her maturity needed to grow with her new persona.

I poured a few fingers into each cup and handed one to the beleaguered woman. "Oh, thanks, Norby. I'm just no good at this stuff. Why the hell does he have to complicate things?" Like Kool Aid, the CC was tossed down her throat, and she beckoned for more. And more.

I listened to her whine and bitch for a half hour on what a miserable piece of shit her husband was, and how much she loved him. In her desperation, she kissed me and we made out awhile before she lost track of what she was doing. I could see the dizzy part wash over her. The euphoric sensation of being drunk on incredibly good whiskey, not giving a shit about anything.

I had dumped my booze into my cup of beer and was nursing it. Noreen zoned out on three more good shots and buzzed herself to sleep. I covered her with a throw cover and left her snoring peacefully.

So much for marital bliss.

I wanted to check with the Pink Power office to see if anything had come down about Rikki. Like the bozo I was, I knew my cell phone was under my dirty underwear, at home. Stu's land line was occupied by a distraught angry blonde gal with great legs. She waved her fist while calling some poor goon a string of nasty names. She gave me a look and scared me away.

I found Isabelle with an audience of horny teenagers, waving her glass of beer to command respect. I had to repeat her name three times to get her attention. Finally, "Oh, hi, Mr. Klein. You and Mom done?" Her smirk was too precious.

"No. Yes. Isabelle, I need to use a phone, but some war lord has taken over the land line. Is there a cell I can use?"

"Sure, you can use Daddy's." Clutching her beer, she pranced away, leaving her subjects staring after her. I tried small talk, but the boys were stoned and made no sense that I could figure out, other than, "Oh, like wow, man."

She came back just as cheerful, handing me the cell phone. She was stoned.

Oh, shit, and with the Chief of Police in the house. Well, little Isabelle was happy, and I was gone. I stepped outside and ran into a basket of sweet smelling delight, slender arms, long curvaceous legs, flat belly, bubble ass, and just too too perfect hoo hoos. "Dr. LaRioux." What?

Her lips parted and heaven opened with them. "Mr. Klein, what a pleasant surprise. Are you here to support the candidate?"

"No, not me. It's the free beer and a chance to get his wife drunk. I didn't take you for the political type."

She stepped up to the top step to my level and stood seriously close. Now what do I do?

"He's your friend isn't he? Don't you think it would be nice to offer your support? Hmmm?"

She tilted her head waiting for an answer, but my tongue was too hard to speak.

Then, to confirm that I really was a mindless idiot, she slipped her fingers behind the buttons to my shirt, and pulled me down the steps. She spoke as I stumbled along with her, "I'm here to make a contribution. You know, lawn signs and brochures. I can do that later. First we need to talk."

Talk? Lawn signs? Yeah, I can see it now in bright blue and white, "Vote For Stu-pid."

Leading me like a puppy to a silver Beemer convertible, she opened the door and pushed me in. By the time my mind decided this was not going to be another wet dream, she was ripping down the street taking a corner at what must have been mach-speed. The flesh on my face had been pulled back by the g-forces. I finished my beer CC combo and tossed the cup.

I glued my eyes on the pilot of this spaceship, mesmerized by the change in her attitude out of the office. The Louis Vuitton sunglasses perched on her nose did not come from a rack at Wal-Mart. Her legs were doing marvelous things with the way too short gray pencil skirt as she attacked the gas pedal. She was launching us towards an upscale condo, where a block away, the garage door opened. It must have a heat seeking sensor on it.

What in the hell was going on?

CHAPTER
TWENTY

● ● ● ● ● ● ● ● ● ● ● ● ● ● ● ● ● ● ● ●

LANDING IN HER ASSIGNED GARAGE SPOT, I needed to know what was happening. Kidnapping was a federal offense, and I had to piss off my only FBI connection. "Ariel—Dr. LaRioux…"

"Don't talk so much. Come on before I realize what a monstrous mistake this is." Mistake?

I followed the clacking of her high heels to the elevator, which opened as we approached. More heat seeking devices. Inside, she punched a button and pushed me against the wall. The Louis Vuitton's were pushed to the top of her head, and she was nuzzling her nose into my neck. "Ariel, uh, what?"

In an effort to make me feel good, she told me, "You know, for a disgusting man, you have a childish sex appeal."

"Ariel, are you sure you have the right person here. It's me, Norby. What are we doing?"

"Don't be so stupid, I'm seducing you. Work with me, dammit."

She left her shoes in the elevator, headed towards a large double door of the penthouse. I didn't belong here. The foyer would swallow my apartment, the Pink Power office, and leave room for my car. The haste she was moving at could have been to get this over with as soon as possible.

Following the trail of flimsy articles of clothing, the first of which was the gray pencil skirt wrapped around her butt and legs. The blouse, a tiny lacy bra, and last but by no means least, an item made of black lacy string with a silk triangle attached to it. I had already fantasized her in a thong. Oh, yeah.

What took place for the next three hours would go untold in detail. I wasn't certain I saw all of it anyway. I was too busy smelling, licking, sucking, caressing, and kissing whatever she placed in front of me. I assumed she was a real life doctor and had training in CPR, but I couldn't catch my breath to tell her I was dying.

106

This scenario wouldn't be complete without sharing a shower with her to wash off the aftermath. This glass cubical had six strategically placed sprayers, some pulsating, some twirling, the rest just spraying. She attacked me again and I lay in the puddle on the floor gasping. What she did next will remain a secret. Fifty shades of awesome.

There was a glass-walled room off the kitchen filled with plants and heat lamps. I was thrown into a chaise lounge where she sat on my lap, and yes, we were both buck naked. Me, a hairy extinct caveman, and Dr. Ariel LaRioux, a goddess transported from the exotic isle of Themyscira. I knew, I just knew that at any moment, Artemis, Athena, Demeter, Hestia, and Aphrodite were going to swing in on golden ropes and kill me. After what I just experienced, I didn't care. Take me.

The goddesses must be waiting, because all we were doing now was sipping snifters of Drambuie, staring at each other. Testing the water, I reach up and touch one of her private things. Her response was to dribble the scotch liqueur on my chest, let it run down my body, and lick it off. Another shower.

It was dark now, and she fell asleep in my arm on her memory-foam bed. In the morning, I woke up alone. Nothing new to me. She came in wearing a silk robe thing, not bothering to tie it. All the blood had run out of my arm where she had been lying, and it was stinging like holy shit.

The coffee she brought in was an aphrodisiac, smelling so good. "Good morning, Mr. Klein. Sleep well?"

I looked at her, "I'm Mr. Klein again?"

She gave me that "Hmmm!" again.

I guzzled the coffee, not daring to ask for more, and she didn't offer. "Ariel, what was all that about?"

"Hmmm?"

"Don't give me that noncommittal hmmm crap, Ariel. You fucked my brains out last night, and you didn't get what you wanted because I'm still here. Be nice and spill it. What?"

She pouted her whisper, "The bonds Norby. The bonds. Why else would I screw a repulsive mess like you?"

"Ariel, I already told you there are no bonds."

The silky robe thing slid off, piling on the floor, while she slithered across the bed to accost me again. She slid over me, her lips painting my face with spit. Yes, that's seductive.

My ear was being sucked like a Popsicle, while she whispered, "You and me, Norby. We can take the bonds and disappear. There's a small island in the Caribbean we can live on. Rum and coconuts. Just us."

"I'll take the island idea, Dr. LaRioux, but it'll have to be on your credit card. Ariel, there are no bonds. Go back to whoever told you to whore me out and set them straight."

The next thing I knew I was standing naked in the foyer with my clothing on the floor, in front of the elevator. Nothing new to me. I had myself assembled in quick time before anyone would step off the elevator. Maybe her next victim. Or the connection she had in the Duluth police department.

Outside, I was greeted by a typical Duluth dose of weather—drizzle and cold. I had about ten bucks in my pocket, plus change. My only connection to safety was Stu's cell phone, still in my pocket, so I called a cab.

The cab's timing was perfect. He waited to arrive just as I was starting to become saturated. I thought a woodpecker was rapping on the back of my head, but it was my teeth chattering. I think I mentioned cold. "Where to, Mac?" I climbed in and stuttered Rikki's address. The cabbie didn't trust me to come back so he followed me to her apartment where I picked up the gray, smelly, over-weight, hair ball cat. Next was Stu's address. The tab came to $9.90, so my chauffer got a ten cent tip in change. I offered the cat, and he answered in a string of insults all very new to me. I absorbed his outrage and got out in front of my Plymouth Reliant, right where I left it.

The rain had mottled on the windshield, but I could see inside the car good enough. Oh, shit. My first call was to Jeanine. "Honey, I'm at Stu's house. You better come and pick me up."

"Jesus, Norby, pick yourself up. Or won't that piece of crap car start?"

"Yeah, I'm pretty sure it'll start, but there's a dead guy inside."

CHAPTER
TWENTY-ONE

● ● ● ● ● ● ● ● ● ● ● ● ● ● ● ● ● ● ●

My next call was to the 911 dispatcher, and with the mention of Detective Lieutenant Grosslein's house as a location for a homicide, it took about three minutes for the first responder to arrive. Two more minutes and the street looked like a Fourth of July celebration.

The cat was hanging from my arm, oblivious to the mist collecting on it. I had to shake it to be certain it was alive.

I answered all the questions, four times, and told them that, yes, I knew the victim, but not his name, and the cat belonged to a friend. Why would they give a shit about the cat? I'd supply the victim's name in a few minutes. The ME dragged the body out and laid him on a gurney. Even with the piano wire digging deeply into his neck, I recognized the pimply kid that had been making out with Isabelle.

One of the detectives motioned to me, so I stepped to the car. As I passed the gurney with the pimply kid lying on it, I groused at the senseless act and had an idea of what was to come next.

He was sitting in the driver's seat, his feet planted on the pavement. I didn't know the guy, but it was obvious he knew me. Nodding to the steering wheel, he asked, "What's that?"

I leaned over him, careful to not make any contact. I saw his concern, answering, "It's a screw driver. Jammed into the ignition." I looked back at the covered gurney and knew what happened, but was confused as to the reason for it.

As the tow truck backed up to my Reliant, I told the detective, "I'll meet you at the station and make a statement. This whole thing will clear itself up."

It was starting to rain harder.

I walked up to Stu's house, and Jeanine was sitting in her car in front. I dumped the cat in the back seat and motioned her to come with me up to the house. She twisted around with a disgusted look at the cat clawing her upholstery. "Don't worry. It's Rikki's." That information wouldn't replace the upholstery, but at least she knew.

It took a few minutes for the door to open, with a haggard looking Isabelle staring at us. What is it about women who look like hell and still radiate a sexual appeal? Her hair was tossed into a nest an eagle could lay eggs in, her eyes were the color of a whore's lipstick, and her mouth was hanging open, drooling. Hangover. Good, I hoped she felt as bad as she looked.

"Mr. Klein, what is it? What's going on out there?" She glanced at the side show down the street. Then alarmed, she yelped, "Daddy? Is it Daddy? Is he all right?"

"No, Isabelle, it's not Daddy. I'm sure he's hiding in his coffee cup at the station. But I think he might show up soon." The drizzle wasn't letting up so I pushed my way inside, Jeanine following.

Isabelle offered, "Mom is still asleep. Her and Daddy had a big fight last night and he stormed out early. Really mad. Mom was drunk."

"How do you feel, Isabelle?"

"Not very good. Outside, what's going on?" She angled her head at the commotion down the block.

I tried to radiate a calming expression, but was boiling inside. "Isabelle, what's the name of the kid you were making out with yesterday?"

"Steven? Steven Warburg. Why?"

Jeanine started a move to hold the girl while I told her that Steven Warburg had been brutally murdered, but I stopped her. I didn't want a panicked, sick child, with a hung over mother on our hands. "Just need to know, Isabelle. Tell me, was he trying to steal my car yesterday?"

She sat back, relieved. "Oh, that." She grinned. "We thought it would be funny if you went to get your car and it was gone."

Funny? "Isabelle, was anyone else in the game with you?"

"Billy and Mark chickened out and went home. Stevie went out when it got dark. We saw you take off with that woman and knew you'd be gone all night." This thought nourished a giggle from her. "He said he could do it without a key. Is he in trouble?"

"Yeah, he's in trouble. Isabelle, don't go outside. Your dad will be here soon and you can tell him what you told me. Okay?"

"Sure, Mr. Klein." She motioned to Jeanine, "Is this your girlfriend? Is she mad about the other woman?"

I grinned at Jeanine, who answered, "No, I'm not his girlfriend. He's gay and doesn't like girls." I was yanked out of the doorway before I could protest the aspersion on my man-hood.

The cat found fresh upholstery in the front seat, so I tossed it back where it belonged. I had to brush the hair off the passenger seat, and took my rightful place. Evidently, I was the intruder, so the hair ball cat reclaimed his spot on my lap.

Jeanine pulled a U-turn to avoid the confusion where my car used to sit, and went first to a Starbucks, then to the station. Stu was in his office, his head on his folded arms, snoring. The rattling of the glass door brought him to attention. "Huh? What?" He peered at me through two red holes in his face, "Oh, its just you. Go away." He tried to put his head back on his arms, but Jeanine slid a Starbucks under his nose. "Huh? Oh, thanks."

The first sip burned his lip. "Hi, Jeanine. You can stay, but butt head has to go."

She pulled a chair up to his desk and crossed one marvelous jean-covered leg over the other. She glared at him a moment, then said, "Stu, wake up. There's a problem at your house."

He snorted and coffee drooled down his chin. "Yeah, my wife's a drunk and my daughter is . . . well, never mind." Another sip, this one staying in his mouth. "What do you want?"

I started, "Stu, one of Isabelle's boyfriends was playing a prank by trying to steal my car last night."

Stu added, "He'd be doing the neighborhood a favor."

"Stu, he was murdered trying to jam a screw driver in the ignition."

This woke him up. "What? How?"

"From the back seat. Someone was sitting in the back seat, and while he was being impish, a garrote was slung over his head and he was almost decapitated. We talked to Isabelle and she said his name was Steven Warburg. You better get someone over to his house, soon."

The wheels of efficiency took over and the proper actions were put into place. The boy was held for an autopsy, the parents wailed uncontrollably, Isabelle went into hysterics, while Jeanine and I sat watching the tragedy play itself out.

Later in the day, after the paper work and statements, Jeanine and I sat in the Pink Power office waiting for Brew to show up. Jeanine spoke first. "We have to get her now, for good."

Brew stormed in and had just landed her massive frame into a chair, catching the last of Jeanine's comment. "Who? Get who?"

Jeanine had crawled into her business only mode, dead serious. "Kathleen Pierpont. She's killing people who have no business dying. She's a vengeful psychotic maniac and we're going to stop her."

Brew asked, "Where do we start?"

They both looked at me, as if I knew anything. But I did. Part of which I would keep to myself, the rest, I shared. "The feds. We talk to Frank Tellworth and get them in deeper. And, we need to get Rikki out of there."

CHAPTER
TWENTY-TWO

● ●

THE DULUTH FBI OFFICES WERE ANYTHING but pretentious. A handful of generic people, working at generic equipment, doing generic work. It all seemed so mundane. Yet there was an obvious feeling that there was a purpose to it all. The resources at their disposal were mind boggling. I experienced this first hand when I worked with the Minneapolis office in a clandestine operation in Mexico to rescue Marci Hudson's daughter from a sex traffic operation. After I fell in love with my client, Mrs. Hudson, my downward spiral led me to the slums of Duluth. Marci was dead now; so was my spirit. Along with Laura Blake, and my wife, Cheryl.

Rikki was a different story, She wasn't a lover, but someone I loved. She was my pseudo daughter and I needed to get her back on safe ground. I'd lost everyone I'd ever cared about, and I was scared to death that Rikki would be lost. I'd die to keep that from happening.

In Tellworth's office, we got into a lengthy discussion on what to do. Frank's inclination was to put us all in jail to keep us from getting in the way, but he knew better. "Frank, the harbor master, Duane Marglott, has to be a connection to this. Rikki ID'd him as just that, so he must have either been at the Fields house, or mentioned. She also talked about cargo containers holding traffic victims being shipped out. How hard can it be to spot one of those?"

"Believe it or not, Immigration and Customs Enforcement's Homeland Security Investigations is looking at that now. With the hundreds of containers being loaded every day, we can't open all of them. The worst part is scaring the traffickers off to another port. Duluth is a major shipping port for iron ore and grain, so it's ideal for an occasional container of contraband. Not as popular as the coastal ports, less attention is spent here."

Frustrated, I asked, "Well, what's next?"

His answer was what I expected. "For you, nothing. If we need input or help in any way, I'll get to you." I glared at him, and he must have recalled my threat to kill him if anything happened to Rikki. "I know what your concern is, Klein. Maybe your best approach would be to take a closer look at the Fields place." He went to his desk and pulled out a manila envelope. "I knew you'd be in here, anxious to do something about Officer Thielges." He handed the envelope to me. "Here's what we know and some stuff on Burton Fields's brother, Gordon. Give us another week to get our guy to safe ground, then do what you want there. In the long run, your interfering at the house may play into our hands at the docks. Get them on the run, so to speak."

I was starting to burn close to the ignition stage. "A week is too long, Frank. Two days, then we send in the cavalry."

He put his hand up, firm. "No, too soon. Four days."

We stood up, "Four days, then we start shooting."

● ●

NORBERT KLEIN, JEANINE, AND BREW LEFT FRANK Tellworth's office. About ten minutes later he got a call. The muted voice on the other end, "They're gone. Drove off. We bugged their office and put a GPS on the hot babe's car. Jeanine, I think. We couldn't get into Klein's apartment. Some heavy Jewish woman was watching from across the hall. She might just be a nosy neighbor. No problem there."

Agent Tellworth gave an order, "Get our guy out of the Fields house right away. Leave the police plant there as bait." He sat back at his desk thumbing through a confidential report from Homeland Security, on an innocuous cargo container being monitored all the way from Houston, Texas. He locked it in his drawer and picked up the phone again.

There was no answering voice on the other end, yet Frank spoke, "Tell Duane Marglott the shipment is in Iowa right now. Should be here in two days. We've only got four days to bust this open before the civilians get involved. We'll have this wrapped up by then. Tell our contact in the police station that they might be loosing an officer."

CHAPTER
TWENTY-THREE

• •

IN JEANINE'S CAR, I TOLD HER, "LET ME OFF at the precinct house. My car should be ready to go and I want to go home to get my own phone and weapon. This is getting too close to be unarmed."

In an unexpected gesture, Brew spoke from the back seat. "You want me with you? Another set of eyes?"

Her comment mended some of my doubts about her, and it felt good. "Thanks, Brew. I appreciate the offer. Go back to the office and see what you can make out of the shit Tellworth gave us. Keep in mind, it might be a smoke screen to keep us busy. If my car isn't ready, can I call you for a ride?"

Brews affirmative nod was good enough. I opened the door to get out and was warned, "Don't forget your cat."

The normal hub-bub in the station house was at a higher level. I asked the desk sergeant, "What's going on. Sounds like a party."

"They brought in Clete Michaels. Just got done grilling him. He's got nothing. Sounds clean to me."

"Think they'll let me talk to him?"

"Won't hurt to ask." He gave me a long look, and the highly trained mouser hanging from my arm. His comment could be taken a number of ways. "Nice pussy." I ignored him.

Clete Michaels was sitting in an interrogation room, chained to a metal table. He looked like a kid who was caught with his underage cousin. Like I was. The confident aura he normally wore had been stripped away, with just a shell of a man, shaking with fear. Chief Ramsay was talking to a couple of suits I recognized from the DA's office. Protocol would have me wait until they were done talking, they being important, and me being, well, me. I strode up, "Chief, I want to talk to him."

His double take was precious. The two suits gave me a disdaining look wondering if I had just stepped out of rehab. I could help if I was able to get past the pretentious snobbery. Maybe the cat was out of place. I gave it another try, "Chief, I was the target when Angie was hit. He didn't do it. I want to talk to him."

He glanced at the two gentlemen. They laughed at me, and the chief said, "Yeah. Go ahead. We got a mike on in the room, so keep it clean." The protest from the DA's representatives went nowhere.

I stepped into the room and immediately felt my privates freeze. Man, I know the process is to make the perp uncomfortable, but at this temperature, they'd have to thaw him out. I stuck my head out the door and bellowed, "Turn the goddamn heat up in here."

In a moment the radiator started ticking, but not enough. I felt lucky to get that much. I sat across from him, letting hair ball have free run of the table top. "Clete Michaels. You piece of shit, why did you have to treat that woman so bad."

He almost cried, "I didn't kill her. I loved her." Hair ball was licking Clete's face.

"Oh, shut up, you turd. I know you didn't kill her. Not with the rifle anyway. But you would have if she had stuck around any longer." I stood over him, yelling, "You don't fucking hit women, ass hole. You beat the shit out of her and now they think you shot her. Best place for you is in jail with some queenie up your butt with a hundred more waiting to ram you."

His plea went nowhere. "Please, I didn't kill her."

"Fuck you, Clete."

I pulled hair ball from Clete's face and met the chief outside. "He's an ass hole, but he didn't kill Angie. I saw the car drive away and it was way too new for his. It left in no hurry. He would have bolted. The rifle was silenced, and had to have had a night scope. Way over his head. Put out an APB for Kathleen Pierpont. She's the only one with the balls to do it."

I started to turn, but I remembered why I was here in the first place. "Is my car done being dissected? I wanna go home."

The suit obviously more important than the other one spoke, "You seem to be certain he wasn't the shooter."

"Learn to listen, man. Angie was given a facial shot just when she was inches from my face. She was blown up to scare me. The second shot came an inch from my head, on purpose. I'm being played by a psychotic screw job, like a cat with a mouse. When she's tired of playing, she'll get me. The way she wants. In her own damn time."

A uniformed officer came to me, "Here's your keys, Norbs. It's kind of messed up, and the ignition is hanging out of the steering column, but I think it starts."

"Thanks." He said it started. That was a step up.

I found the garage and the hulk of my oxidized maroon Plymouth Reliant. There was finger print dust all over everything, and the driver's backrest was covered with dried blood. All that remained of a curious joke playing kid that got to kiss the lovely Isabelle as his last gesture. Just a game piece to Kathleen, but a dead empty space in the lives of his parents. A lab tech came to me, "Sorry about the mess, but the car is in pretty bad shape anyway. Didn't find any prints, but did get a foot print on the back floor behind the driver's side. A woman's." He handed me a Tyvek tarp to drape over the seat.

"Thanks."

The screw driver used by Steven Warburg that started this insanity, rested on the dash board. I have a hunch it belongs to Stu. I used it to touch the wires draping out of the gutted steering column, and Glory Be, it started.

By the time I got home my hands were black from the print dust left on the steering wheel. I looked down at the passenger side floor mat, leaned over, and carefully picked up a cigarette butt. Unless one of the lab techs was a woman, smoking on the job, I don't know why they missed this. I put it back on the mat thinking it should go to the lab for a DNA run. I already knew it came from the pouting lips of psycho bitch.

I wiped my hands off on my pants and got out in front of my tenement apartment. My original goal was to get my phone and a weapon. Now, I didn't give a shit.

There were no lights outside my building. Either the place was still set up for gas lamps, or the owner thought electricity was just a waste of energy. I stumbled on the bottom step and went into cardiac arrest when the bony hand was placed on my shoulder. "Jeez."

My friend, Hanky, stopped me from screaming. "Shhh. Bad men come and go."

His warning had shades of Bela Lugosi slithering through bat caves and grave yards. I understood he was warning me. Whispering, I leaned closer to be heard, and was stricken by the stench of Duluth sewers wafting from him. "Are they up there now?" Jeez.

He shook his head, muttered, "No, gone," and slunk away to do bonding things with Lugosi.

I crept around to the back, knocking over a metal garbage can. That was it, nice and quiet. I'd done this enough to know where the rest of the traps were, finally getting up to the second floor. I stood in the hallway for a few minutes listening for anything. The silence was broken by the rasping of locks and chains on Mrs. Feldstein's door. She cracked it open, "Psst. Norbert. Here."

Norbert? She knew better than that.

I slid to her door and couldn't decide if the stench from Hanky was worse or better than the garlic pouring from her place. With her finger aside her lips, she whispered, "Some hoodlums were here trying to get into your door. I stared at them and they left. They never got in." She reached for the cat, cooing at the supposed softness, "Oh, little Min-Min." Finished with the coddling, she abruptly handed it back, "Cats no good. Eat and poop."

"Thank you so much, Mrs. Feldstein. How many were there?"

She questioned, "Many?"

Checking my frustration, "Hoodlums. Men. How many?"

"Three."

"What did they look like?"

"Oh, my, what. I don't know how to say. Yiddish, no. German, yah! *Junge männer*. Young. Young men. Office type of young. Should be at work and not prowling around. Oh, I worry about you so much." She squished my cheeks between her calloused hands like I was a sandwich.

"Yeah, that's fine, Mrs. Feldstein. Their shoes. What did their shoes look like?"

"Shoes, schmooze. Who looks at shoes. New. *Neue glänzende schuhe*. Shiny. What?"

"But they never got inside?"

"No, no, they stood around and we gave evil eye to us. They no go in."

"Thank you, honey. Go back inside now. I love you, dear."

One thing about lab technicians, or specialists sent out on jobs they didn't do very often—they never dress for the part. Grab a techie and tell him to go out on a clandestine operation, and it's like a kid on a first date. All thumbs. I scooted back to the Reliant and got my kit out of the trunk.

I carried a beat up satchel in the trunk, hidden in the spare tire hole. I didn't have a spare, so it worked out just fine. I kept an assortment of gadgets and trinkets to make my life easier in touchy situations. Like breaking and entering, or illegal spying, or any other thing that could get me killed. If the super-tech stuff didn't work, I also had a hammer and crowbar.

Upstairs, I waved the nosy Mrs. Feldstein back into her apartment. I flashed a high density beam across the door frame, catching new scratch marks. If the goons who paid me a visit would have just turned the knob they would have been in. I didn't lock it.

Yeah, I know. Give me some slack.

However, if they did get in and didn't know about shutting off the alarm, a siren loud enough to scramble the F-16s at the Duluth 148th Fighter Wing, would have kept them away. I reached behind the refrigerator and flipped the switch on the alarm module. I waited a moment just to be sure. Cool. The cat jumped down, its beacon already on a mouse.

I walked slowly through my one room scanning with the BrickHouse 153-AVD-110, and was convinced the place was clean. I meant in an electronic surveillance sense. My apartment was not clean in a clean way. I liked it this way. Jeez.

If I was a target, there was another. I used my cell and called the Pink Power office. After the Pink Power salutation from Jeanine, I cut in real quick. "Hi, honey, I won't be in for a while. I'm swatting mosquitoes."

There was a brief silence, and my gal understood. "Yeah, I suppose they can be a nuisance." She disconnected and no doubt went about de-bugging the office and telephone. Then she and Brew would check out their homes.

I took Stu's phone out of my pocket and put it in my magic bag of tricks. Like Felix the Cat. I reached under the bed springs and untangled the Sig from the mess of wire holding it in place. Dropping the clip, I was happy to see there was a full load.

Outside, It was dark as the dungeons that Hanky's eyes were nested in. I had enough trouble working in daylight, let alone the dark. I rigged my Talos bomb detector to sense a few things besides an explosive. I clipped it to a telescoping shaft and scanned the under carriage of my Plymouth. I had doubts that there was any exposed metal free enough of grease and road grime to attach a device, but then, I was a man and have been trained to be wrong.

I was and I wasn't. The Talos scanner sent off a faint signal. I crawled under and found a GPS wired to a rusty piece of the body. Back upstairs I fondled the gadget, thinking I could get a better one at Radio Shack. Government cutbacks, I guess. Yup, I was totally certain this came from the toy box at the FBI office. Now what? Pondering that, I got a brilliant flash. Now, where the hell was the damn cat? "Here, kitty, kitty. Here, Hairball. Come to Daddy."

I think I was getting smarter by the minute. I went to the kitchen and scrounged for a can to open. The best I could come up with was a tin of diced rutabagas I got for a food drive about ten years ago. Evidently, I cheated someone out of a good meal. I didn't have an electric can opener, so I made a production of clanking the manual one that barely functioned. Huzzah, huzzah, it worked. Hairball came slouching from behind the cupboard at the sound of a can of food being opened.

My God, this thing was heavy. I hoisted him—I was going to assume it was a male—up to the counter top. The GPS wasn't too big, so I tied it to his collar. As a reward I dumped the rutabagas in a dirty plate sitting in the sink. No, I didn't have any clean ones. Setting it on the floor I watched Hairball turn into a ravenous jungle beast. I had to get more rutabagas.

So, what did we have now? The FBI was interested enough in the Pink Power group to want to know where we went, and who we talked to and about what. I'd never been so honored. They were trying to keep our inept civilian hands out of the cookie jar until they didn't care what we did. They had an operation in place and Tellworth didn't want it mucked up. In my inane way of deciphering the natural course of people's actions, I could usually get to the next phase in time to avoid being killed. My degree in psychology was a joke to some, but oh, so useful to me. That, plus a gut instinct, had allowed me to live this long. The obvious to me now, and I knew I was right, was for Tellworth to use us as a mop-up.

Time to rally the troops and go over the battle plan. I was sure we could think of one.

Back in the Reliant I called Jeanine and agreed to meet at a Perkins located on Miller Highway, not far from the Pink Power office. I made an inference that just the two of us meet, but was admonished with a lecture on learning to get along with Brew, or else. One way or another, Bruin Heinz was going to be a part of this circus. I needed to be congenial, but cautious.

CHAPTER
TWENTY-FOUR

● ● ● ● ● ● ● ● ● ● ● ● ● ● ● ● ● ● ●

JEANINE WAS ALONE IN THE BOOTH. I sat down with a flourish, asking, "No Brew? I thought you were so adamant on including her."

She had that serious look planted on her face. I waited until she opened up. "I told her you were not excited about her being involved. She was really hurt, Norbs. She thought you and her were on a trusting basis now. She said she'd wait while I talked to you first."

Jeanine leaned towards me, in a lower voice, "Norby, if you don't learn to play with the other kids, both Brew and I will go home. If we aren't a team, lives will be lost. I know this all stems from your fear about Rikki getting hurt, and you need to understand that we all have the same dread. Brew is an amazingly talented woman, and frankly, I'd rather go in with her than you. Some day, you're going to listen to some of the jobs she's been on. Impressive."

I knew all of this and had no argument.

The Perkins waitress brought us coffee, and when we didn't order food we got the eye rolling routine, before she swished away. I tried to make my point, "I don't really know what it is, Jeanine, there's something about your Amazon friend that bothers me."

Her response was just what I deserved, "Well, wah, wah. Get over it. You want Rikki out or not?"

We argued for about a half hour before feeling guilty enough to at least order pancakes to appease the waitress. I'd know Jeanine a long time and had gone through some harrowing experiences with her. She was like a sister to me and because of that bond we could read each other like a book. I knew there was more she was holding back.

By the sigh she pushed through her lips, and the hanging head ordeal, I felt she was coming close to a mind-blowing revelation. Had I known where it was headed I would have let it alone. She moved from across the table to sit beside me. Maybe she wanted to fondle me. I dunno.

Her cell phone lay on the table. She draped her napkin over it, then cupped her hand on it. I guessed she was connected to somebody outside. It had to be Brew.

Leaning into my ear, the good one, she spoke softly, "What I'm going to tell you is going no further than that pill of a brain in your head. If you spout this to anyone, including Brew, I'll pack up and leave you forever. Understand?"

"Sounds serious. Is she listening to us?"

Jeanine glanced at the muted phone, "Yes."

"Yeah, okay, I understand. Spill it."

"Brew started life as a man. She's had a sex change operation. She's embarrassed and wants you to be able to accept her for what she is. Understand?"

Oh, shit. I had sex with her. Him. It. "What?"

All I got as a response was a stern look.

I sputtered, "She told me she was raped as a kid."

"She was. Assaulted by a gang of guys who almost tore his penis off because he was gay. The operation came later."

"Yeah, but . . ."

She moved back to her side of the table, I was left with my face hanging open, and we ate pancakes. Oh, shit.

With syrup dripping down her chin, she muffled through a pound of pancake in her mouth, "Now, will you be decent to her?"

"I had sex with . . ."

"Her, Norby. She's a her. Say it. She's a her."

"Her. I had sex with her." Jeez.

Jeanine was up leaning over the table with a sticky fork clutched in her fist. If I didn't comply I was going to become a shish-kabob. "Okay, her. She's a her. Don't kill me. I said it." This was going to call for heavy amounts of alcohol to become clear to me, but not at Perkins Family Restaurant. "Jeanine, I said it. Now sit down. People are staring."

"Those people are going to call an ambulance if you fuck this up."

I put my hands up in surrender. "Okay, you win. I'll be nice." Still, I found the idea of having sex with a person not originally born as a woman, very—different.

I didn't stand a chance. I lay my head on the table, locking my fingers behind my head. I gave up.

While my brain was spinning, Jeanine uncovered the phone and spoke softly into it. A moment later our gigantic partner strode up to our table, sliding in next to Jeanine. I was right, she was sitting outside all this time.

Not one single other person in this restaurant was aware of Brew's sexual orientation. Nobody was aware of her being a private investigator, ex-CIA, and who knows what else. The oddity that gets people to at least take a look was not her size. She was a beautiful arrangement of blonde, hoo-hoos, butt, arms, and legs. When she was dressed skimpily, her muscles were the attraction. Tonight people stared because she, herself, was the attraction. Yes, she was beautiful.

A new pot of coffee came, and Brew shifted her gaze between me and Jeanine.

She locked in on Jeanine for a long time, then cleared the air. "You covered the phone. You tell him about me?" Her glare was hard, which would frighten anyone else. And me.

Jeanine sighed, "I had to, honey. Sorry, but we're too close to keep secrets. Are you upset?"

"Yes, but it had to come out at some point. I don't care anymore." She looked at me with that fierce look, "How about you?"

In spite of what I've just learned, and the persona she displayed, I could see the years of hurt in her eyes. The trauma and ridicule she grew up with, the confusion of not knowing who or what she was. I was way beyond the 'apology and walk careful' routine. "Brew, I don't give a shit. You are who you are and that's fine. We're a team and you know that my only concern is Rikki. After, we'll get blasted on Jack Daniels again, and who knows, maybe a celebratory roll in the sheets again."

I looked up and Brew had poured me a fresh cup. "Thanks. But I don't think I'll be rolling with you again. Sorry if I said anything disparaging. This is not a comfortable situation for me right now."

You know how sometimes you got a flash in your mind that seemed to settle outrageous ideas? Well, just then, I had the flash of John Lithgow in the movie, *The World According to Garp*, run through my head, and everything started to look a whole lot more normal.

So, all that was settled, and Brew dismissed me with a wave of her hand. Evidently, whatever problem I posed became a moot point. She looked at Jeanine, and said, "We have to get Rikki out of that house. Can we trust Bozo here? He's not going to get wimpy is he?" She looked at me and I expected bullets to come blasting out of her eyes, or her finger tips. Looking at her eyes it hit me that in spite of what I just learned, she was a babe. A man, yeah, but a babe, and I had sex with . . . her.

I gave her my most endearing smile, "I'm okay. Let's get started. Did you find any bugs? In the office? Home? Car?"

Brew answered, "The office phones and one under each desk, as well as the conference room. They left your desk alone."

My feelings were hurt. "Sure, I didn't get a bug because they thought my desk was just a storage place."

"Wa-wa-wa. Get over it. Our home phones were bugged also. There was no GPS on our cars. They couldn't get into your apartment so all they had was your piece of crap car."

"It's paid for."

Jeanine broke in, "All right, you two, play nice. What next?"

My logic was working, prompting, "Where are the bugs you took out?"

Brew set a paper bag on the table, and like a Halloween goody bag, I shoveled through looking for the good stuff. "All cheap second-grade crap like the one on my car. We don't even warrant a first-class clandestine operation. First thing tomorrow we have to swarm all over Tellworth's office to get him to unload his plans."

CHAPTER
TWENTY-FIVE

● ● ● ● ● ● ● ● ● ● ● ● ● ● ● ● ● ● ●

FIRST THING THE NEXT MORNING, JUST LIKE I SAID, much earlier than most civil employees are used to starting their day, we stormed into the Duluth FBI office. I had expected an armed guard, or at least a big menacing guy, to stop us, but the only interference was a bespectacled woman with mousy brown hair. She had to have been used to intrusions and didn't bother becoming alarmed. Her simple, "Yes? May I help you?"

Jeanine smiled with her curt look, "Just tell Agent Tellworth he's being invaded."

By the time she reacted, we were encroaching his space. He looked up, and his lack of surprise surprised us. "Come in. Coffee?"

His phone rang and his response was, "Yes, Caroline, they're in here. Thank you. Could you bring in coffee for four, please? And a plate of scones? Thank you."

He smiled and said, "I was expecting you. Please, sit."

Caroline was prompt with the coffee and scones, asking if we needed anything else. Except for answers from Tellworth, no, we needed nothing.

I tossed the bag of spooks on his desk, and started, "You planted bogus gear to get our attention. Rather childish, don't you think, Frank?"

He sat back munching a scone. "Childish, yes. And the work of amateurs. Not my intention at all. But when amateurs are sent out, we get an amateurish job. I apologize. All the experienced agents are busy on another operation, so I mistakenly used people not accustomed to outside work. They're all being disciplined. But, it may work to our advantage to have you involved."

He looked at me, "I didn't forget the warning you gave me Norby. While upset, it illustrated how sincere you were, and I knew you'd react after you saw the mess we made of trying to bug you all."

"Make it clean and simple, Frank. Tell us what's going on."

He sat forward. I ignored the crumb of scone clinging to his lip. "What we know, is that the Fields house is the gathering place for the traffickers, and the Fields are held as captives. Also, human traffic is coming in cargo containers from various points, shipping out to foreign ports for the purpose of slavery. Mainly young women, some children. Anyone older wouldn't have the stamina to survive. We've been tracking containers and have finally got one in sight that is coming here. Supposedly, a common carrier was commissioned, but we put one of our agents behind the wheel. Unfortunately, his co-driver is on their side, so communication is hard to get out to us."

He finally found the crumb, looked at it, and tossed it in the waste basket. He missed. For whatever reason, I suddenly thought about, Hairball, Rikki's mangy cat. I had to get a poop box for him.

He went on. "So, that's where all our experienced agents are. Watching the harbor freight coming in."

Jeanine spoke up, "What about Duane Marglott, the harbor master?"

Tellworth was silent for a moment, then revealed, "He's ours. In order to get ingrained with the traffickers he's had to do some things that were, shall we say, shady. Believe it or not, we've working on this thing for seven years, and we aren't going to blow it now."

Brew's turn to be logical, "You said we could be helpful. How?"

He leaned back, steepled his fingers, and looked very thoughtful. "When the container comes in, the dock crew is going to be busy taking care of it. With most of them out of the Fields house, I want you to storm it. Get Officer Thielges and the Fields out safely."

My turn, "How will we know, and how much time will we have?"

"You'll need all three of you to get into the house at the same time, armed. There will have to be a lookout stationed who will call you when the container comes in. We aren't going to do it because we absolutely do not want any communication from us to get into the hands of the wrong people."

Jeanine again, "Which berth will the container drop at?"

"There's no way to predict that."

Jeanine spoke up, "We need some indication so we don't mount our horses and invade a house full of dock workers. If there's a better way to screw up your operation, I can't think of one. Besides, you want us at the house to keep us out of your way at the dock." There are times like this that I appreciate her wisdom more than I can ever express. I'd give her a big old kiss, but she'd just hurt me.

He became pensive for a moment, then said, "Give me a cell number, and I'll call when it hits the fan. It could happen at any time from right now or up to a week. So, you have to be in position to move quickly." This was longer than the original four days and I didn't like it.

We all exchanged thank-yous, gave Caroline a nod for being a good gopher, and gathered outside. The traffic was buzzing all around us and we didn't have a clue as to what came next. Since Jeanine refused to ride in my car, we sat in hers, which was somewhat insulated from the Duluth traffic noise. Then, I remembered why I became a PI. Because I was just so damn smart.

I was relegated to the back seat because that was where the two girls thought I belonged. I leaned over the front seat to lay out my idea. In doing so I came close to Brews cheek, wondering if she ever had to shave. Anyway, I told them, "Jeanine, take a drive up Brighton Beach Road past the Fields house. We have to find a camping spot."

Brew turned to me with that threatening look. "We aren't sleeping in a tent."

"A tent? How primitive. No, don't you remember the old Winnebago I got after the Pierpont case was closed? I've got it in storage. All we need to do is get some gas, fill it with water and propane. Maybe pump up a couple tires."

Jeanine turned and asked, "You sure it'll start, Norbs?"

"Of course it'll start. Have some faith."

She threatened me with, "It better start and if the bathroom isn't working you know what I'm going to do to you."

Ouch. "Yes, dear, I'm well aware of what you are capable of doing."

"Okay then. I'll drop you off at home and you get what you need and we'll find you out on Stoney Point Drive."

Back at my place, I stepped out of the car and Brew stopped me cold, quietly adding to my fear. "Klein, don't fuck this up."

I was about getting tired of the warnings and threats, so I cut back with, "Back off, Brew. If you've got something to settle, we'll take care of it when Rikki's safe. Until then, we're on the same team. Don't forget that."

She knew I was serious and kept her mouth shut.

I leaned in the passenger window, talking over Brew's body to Jeanine, "You two go get whatever you need, and meet me out on Stoney Point Drive. Better bring both of your cars, and raid the weapons bin. We're going to need some fire power. And we'll need flak jackets."

Jeanine yelled at me, "I just said all that, you bone head."

I love and understand Jeanine, but I had a feeling that when this ordeal was over I was going to have a serious problem with Brew. I hoped I was smart enough to stay alive through it.

Back in the apartment, I threw together what I thought would be good enough for an assault, grabbed the cat, and told the Plymouth where to take us. Like a good car, we stopped in front of the storage depot I rented.

CHAPTER
TWENTY-SIX

● ●

I SWUNG OPEN THE STORAGE DEPOT DOORS to reveal the stately form of my 1985 Winnebago twenty-four-foot Chieftain. Man, what a beauty this was, and still is. 454 monstrous cubic inches of engine that could never get enough gas to make it truly happy. I had enough forethought to keep a battery charger on it permanently, so starting was no problem. It was the dirt, cobwebs, grime from the last trip, busted muffler, low tires, leaky ceiling in the bathroom, and mold in the refrigerator that the girls may find offensive.

It took about an hour of the best cleaning I had ever done to make it ship-shape. After copious amounts of starter fluid dumped into the carburetor, the engine coughed, wheezed, spit, and rumbled to life. Lumbering to the corner service station I treated the old war wagon to new air in the tires, a full tank of gas, and a propane charge. Oh, yeah, the radiator was almost empty. Oil? I had to buy a case just to be sure.

The next stop was to the liquor store for enough beer and ice to keep us all healthy while we waited for our orders to commit mayhem.

● ●

ON THE WAY TO STONEY POINT DRIVE, I passed the Fields mansion, wondering what was going on inside. My thoughts were constantly on Rikki and how she was being treated. I slowed down but didn't dare hesitate. There had to be a guard or lookout stationed someplace. I took a right at Stoney Point, following the lakeshore. The waves were up today, but not too bad. Gazing out across the wasteland of space that made up the huge body of water, the end of the world was surely out there at the edge of nothingness. Or, at least the UP of Michigan.

I picked a gravelly spot across the road from the lake that the Winnebago could back into without being seen too readily from the road. Tossing a few boards under the right side wheels, it was leveled good enough. I let the cat out to dump whatever it had stored up, and set up a lawn chair, cracked open a beer and waited. And waited. Then waited some more. Starting to worry, it was getting dark and they might not see me nestled in the bushes. My beer of choice this trip had been Lost Lake, a mellow pilsner brewed in Wisconsin. At ten bucks a case, it would taste good enough. I pulled the tab on my fourth when two sets of headlights pulled into the camping spot. I felt relieved, until the two girls got out and started ragging on me for about six-hundred infractions of decency, common sense, and male frailties.

Jeanine saw the cat and started the ragging all over.

I don't think I brought enough beer.

I sat and watched them unload enough equipment, clothing, feminine supplies, and food to stock a Wal-Mart. One of the big ones. I burped.

They ensconced themselves in the motor home and I thought they were fighting with each other. However, that's just the way they talked when they set out to sanitize the filth I expected them to live in. Jeez. I sat in the lawn chair with Hairball on my lap waiting for the sanitation process to finish. Running my fingers through his matted hair, I thought about Rikki again, and all of a sudden this damn mangy cat became more important to me. It belonged to her, and now I'd take care of it no matter what.

In 1985, the Winnebago Corporation built this particular model to accommodate six sleeping adults. Eight if two of them were cozy with each other. One would think that since there were only three people here that there would be room for all of us. But, the female mind worked on a different level than motor home designers. The space that Jeanine and her gigantic friend consumed left me with the passenger seat as the only bed left. The answer to my question, "Why do you need so much room?" came out as, "Where else do we put our stuff. Shut up and go to sleep."

Jeez.

Living in a confined space for an extended period of time, with two females who could at any moment, take my life or mash my manhood, was a daunting task. For the first three days I tried to coexist with my business partners, engaging in conversation that made absolutely no sense at all. Topics of debate included the color of nail polish with a blue purse, Lindsey Lohan being prettier than Miley Cyrus, the merits of mushroom soup in a green bean casserole, methods of avoiding menstrual discomfort, and one I still don't understand—female ejaculation.

Once, I made an attempt to extol a comparison between Aaron Rodgers, Payton Manning, and Brett Favre, but backed down by Brew spouting the lifetime records of each one, and an analysis of each. Oh, man. It turned out she was an avid Packer fan, swamping me with an Aaron Rodgers bio. She uttered a claim to entertaining a good portion of the Packers defensive line one night. Huh?

While the white caps on the estrogen in the camper were causing a tidal wave, I pulled out the awning and sat in my lawn chair, listening to, and watching the rain wash the earth clean. I wished it was that simple with life. Always a good time to enjoy a cup of coffee with Hairball on my lap, I noted a few leaks in the awning that could use a duct tape patch. Rikki was always on my mind, another worry to swallow.

We had spent a few constructive hours checking the weapons and gear, and really did have a plan of attack. We had two cars to launch the invasion with. Since I was most dispensable, I would barge in with the first car, while the shock troops took up the rear. The motor home was just too bulky to do any good. The plan was to move in as quietly as possible with me and Brew punching our way into the front door. Jeanine would get to the back and shoot at anything that left that way.

There was no doubt that we had been relegated to the sideline to get us out of the way. I could have placed a winning bet that Agent Tellworth had us under observation. Either by one of the few cars that cruised by, or satellite, or a fishing boat, which to me was but a speck on the horizon, or the small Piper Cub that kept circling overhead. Jeez. Why not drag a banner behind, I SEE YOU.

I had the ability to drink beer and pee it out all night long, never getting more than a mild buzz. Hard booze was another story. The supply of Lost Lake was running low, and I was faced with making a liquor run, or switch to Old Mister Boston. I wanted to stay in focus and opted for the more beer idea. I was about to walk out to the road to flag down the fed's car when it made the daily run past our camp site. I'm sure they would bring a couple cases back.

Standing outside the camper, contemplating my next stupid move, I froze in place when my cell phone chirped inside. From my post under the leaking awning I heard Jeanine, inside, answer, "What!"

I tore open the door, missing the top step, and clattered back to ground zero. I recollected my dignity and was in time to catch her saying, "Yeah, fine, right away." Brew was frozen like me, intent on the phone call. Jeanine closed the phone, "They're moving. Time to rock and roll."

CHAPTER
TWENTY-SEVEN

● ●

SPENDING SO MUCH TIME IN THE CONFINES of the Winnebago, our living conditions got a little messy. And smelly. Clothing was strewn about, mysterious feminine products were left sitting where they shouldn't be, and general disorder became our routine. On more than one night, from my bed in the front seat, I heard the passions of Brew and Jeanine doing things I won't go into. A dirty Go-Girl lay under the kitchen table. What?

The weapons were stored in a large canvas pouch kept in the bath tub. Brew picked it up like it weighed no more than her compact, and dragged it outside. While we worked, Jeanine told us, "We're to sit on the road a couple hundred yards before the Fields driveway. When they leave for the docks we count to a hundred and move in. There should be two black SUVs and the Subaru."

I climbed into the Skylark Jeanine had brought, and the two ladies followed in Brew's Cavalier. Just about far enough up the road to stay out of sight, we pulled to the shoulder and took turns watching the driveway entrance through binoculars. Another check of weapons. I had my Sig tucked into my waistband, a Ruger p95 was nestled in a shoulder holster, and I tucked a Colt AR-15 under my arm. I felt very comfortable with this baby and the 800 rounds a minute that it could spit out the muzzle at 3,200 feet a second. Who'd argue with that! I had it fitted with a 14.5-inch barrel, just long enough to get good range, and easy to maneuver.

Jeanine had a Ruger attached to her belt, and slung an AK 47 over her shoulder. Brew carried a twelve gauge sawed off semi auto, and with one who knew how to use it, that was one of the meanest weapons available. She had a bandolier of twelve-gauge shells slung over her shoulder, and she looked like Rambo. She was carrying 00 buck for the first two shells, then a couple slugs, followed by two more 00 buck. With an eighteen-inch barrel, from twenty-feet, it'd cut anything in half. I didn't catch the handguns she had picked, but there were at least two strapped to her. There was a small bulge under her shirt at the small of her back, and I knew one of her favorites was a Beretta 21A Bobcat. Just a .22, but again, deadly in an experienced hand.

All right, we were armed and waiting. I felt strange in all of this. What we were doing bordered on insanity, not to mention totally illegal and dangerous. Next Halloween I know what I'm going as.

Our nerves were plugged in to high voltage, and I could imagine what would happen if a wandering Highway Patrol were to stop and ask what we were doing. We were standing on the gravel shoulder watching Brew watch the driveway. My nervous system was going to go into spasms, until suddenly, Brew's arm shot out, pointing. "There they go." Sure as hell, just like Tellworth said, two black SUVs, then the Subaru.

Mount 'em up and move 'em out. Yahoo—Rawhide. We crawled into our cars, under the burden of our firepower, and rolled, not too fast, up to the Fields driveway entrance. I slowed down to make sure there were no other vehicles coming out. At the entrance, I punched it and ripped across the lawn, away from the big living room window. There was no doubt that someone was in there watching us, getting their own arsenal into action.

Using the cars as shields, we stopped and crouched, watching the front of the house. We needed to move fast, and we weren't doing it. I hoisted the AR to my shoulder and moved in, watching for the unknown.

Jeanine gave me the signal, and I watched her swiftly creep around to the rear. In my rush to the front door, I checked to be sure Brew was still with me, and slid up to the objective. About three feet away, it swung open and a large shotgun barrel was stuck out. Not willing to go into negotiations here, I opened up with the AR and the door splintered with a dead guy sprawled behind it. I looked down at the bloody dismantled body of Gordo, pleased as punch, stepped over him and moved into the house.

I sensed the movement to my left, and felt the force of Brews 00 buck shot ripping human flesh to shreds. The heat from the blast tore across my back, pushing me further in. Two for us and zero for them. I gave her a thumbs up. A third figure came running down the steps and sprayed a run of 7.62 Russian loads into the floor of the foyer. By the time I got turned, the two slugs in Brews scatter gun disseminated the guy. I looked down and one of his Russian loads had grazed the sole of my shoe. Oh, shit.

I motioned Brew upstairs and went deeper into the house, down here. She had saved my ass twice now, and I hoped I wouldn't need her again. She bound up the staircase, three at a time, and disappeared.

Two gun shots came from the back of the house. It was too loud to be from Jeanine's AK47 and that scared the shit out of me. Upstairs, three more blasts from Brew's cannon shook the house. I ran to the back and heard an engine start, then the roar of what had to be an ATV. That wasn't good.

The back screen door lay cockeyed from one hinge, yawning open. I was in time to see a red ATV sail through the tall brush at the rear of the property. The engine was whining for mercy as the driver was pushing it over the limit. The driver. The tall blonde driver. With the well rounded ass that I, at one time had my face buried in. Kathleen Pierpont.

Jeanine was sprawled on the ground clutching her weapon, bleeding to death. It took me a nano-second to get to her and cushion her head in my arm. I fumbled for my cell until Brew took it from my trembling hand. I heard, "Need a med-evac at the Fields house. There's room to land at the back where a woman has been shot. Make it stat and send all available units."

Brew knelt in the grass on the other side and went to work on the crimson flood soaking Jeanine's chest. She worked fast and efficiently finding whatever pressure points were needed. Talking calmly and smoothly, I guessed she had done this before. "You're okay here, honey. Just a scratch. We got the bastards, babe. I love you, you know."

Through my own flood of fear and tears, I saw Brew crying like a baby as she performed her own brand of magic on my dying partner. Jeanine's eyes fluttered as her lips quaked. She was realizing how badly she was hit and was frightened. I kissed her forehead.

The thumping of the chopper overwhelmed the scene. A crew of white shirts and stethoscopes took over. Four Duluth squad cars screamed into the driveway, and the yard became a circus. The gurney was hauled into the chopper, and Jeanine was gone to the best possible help available. Brew grabbed my arm, dragging me upstairs.

Stu Grosslein had come with the circus, and he and two officers followed us up to a bedroom. We stepped over the remnants of another human, slipping in the gore. Burton Fields was slumped in a wooden chair, a small neat hole in his forehead. Mrs. Fields sat tied to another chair sobbing uncontrollably. I stepped to her and had to make her forget her dead husband and the horror that had consumed her life. I held her head while a cop cut her loose. I hated to intrude on her like this, but I had to. Softly, "Gloria, please, tell me. The girl, Rikki, where is she?"

She looked up at me, sobbing, "Gone. They took her with." That was all I got. The EMT gave her a dose of LaLa land, and she slumped into a far better place. She was carried out, and I suspected she was going to have a long tough road ahead of her.

CHAPTER
TWENTY-EIGHT

● ● ● ● ● ● ● ● ● ● ● ● ● ● ● ● ● ● ●

Brew and I were nice enough to cover a few details with Detective Lieutenant Stu Grosslein, before we took off. The rest could be unthreaded by Agent Tellworth. Stu was in a daze, stumbling around with his mouth hanging open. We stepped aside to make room for the body bag containing Burton Fields. The CSI crew and the ME were taking more pictures than were taken all during World War II. A constant array of light show pyrotechnics to log and record every single detail. Stu was in a fog so we walked away with him fumbling for words that would keep us from leaving. Even if he could talk we would have left anyway.

I followed Brew outside and waited while she retched her stomach into Mrs. Fields azaleas. She pulled her shirt up and wiped her face with the bottom of it. We stood by the Cavalier, where she reached inside and pulled out a pack of Winston. "I didn't know you smoked."

She ignored me and handed over the crumpled pack. I didn't smoke either, but it seemed like a good thing to do. I lit up, and it was. It was wonderful. Her hands were shaking, and she tried to hold them still, and failed. I stepped to her and put my fingers over hers and held tight. The Winston fell out of her lips and she broke up completely. I put my arms around her and she immediately became my friend. We had bathed in blood together and watched our friend get torn up. We were bonded like nobody else had a right to be bonded. From this point on we would protect each other to the death.

Finally, she sniffed, and pushed away. Her words were simple and she knew the feeling as much as I did. "I love you, Norbs." It took a lot for her to say it, but it was sincere. All I needed to do was nod in agreement.

Dusk was settling in and the yard was lit up like a night ball game, the crowd getting bigger. I told her, "We need to get to the hospital and check on Jeanine." Rikki was tearing my mind apart and I hated to choose between the two. In the unlikely event that it was true, I took a chance and prayed. I asked for mercy on Rikki while we went to Jeanine.

Brew got into the passenger seat of the Cavalier, "You drive. I'm kind of fucked up right now." She destroyed two more Winstons before one got ignited. One long drag and it was gone. Amazing suck power.

As evening drew on us, the drama in the hospital became intense. For some reason, all emergency room traffic had to happen at once. The ER was filled with people who had but one goal, to see a doctor. The ER staff ran around like an old MASH unit, but eventually, everybody would survive and go home.

I flashed my complimentary police badge and wedged us up to the reception desk. The haggard clerk looked up and asked the obvious. "What do you want?"

"A woman was brought in with gunshot wounds. We're going to see her. Point to the place she is." I was determined to get beyond all of this and get to where we needed to be.

Her face sank, "Oh, that one. She's in the OR. Follow me."

She was being cordial and helping. I wanted to kiss her. Led to the elevator, she pushed a button, "Second floor. Tell the duty nurse who you are."

About four o'clock the next morning, some dude in a green scrub suit woke us up. Brew, being the one with the most control just sat staring at him. I, being just the opposite, jumped up, "Huh, what, how, tell me?"

He put his arms out to keep me from jumping on him. "I'm Dr. MacKay. She'll be in ICU for about a week. A lot of damage was done and it's not likely she'll walk on her own again. You might as well go home because there won't be any visitors for a few days." He offered the obligatory, "I'm sorry," and walked away.

Outside, Brew took out her cell phone and stepped away from me. The shivers went up my spine again. At this stage, I didn't want any private conversations by anyone. She closed the phone and demanded, "Give me the keys. I'll take you to Jeanine's car. It's still at the Fields house."

"How do you know that? Who'd you just talk to?" I got in but all I got was nothing from her. "Brew, what's going on? For Christ sake don't squirrel out on me now."

Her voice had an edge to it, but she was calm and deliberate. "Nothing. Nothing is going on. Just go home and get some sleep. I'll probably camp out at the hospital tomorrow. I'll see you there."

The scene at the Fields house was winding down with just a few patrol cars and a couple police vans. The yard was dark, save for the early morning glow from the east. It was a cold and desolate morning, starting to mist. I remembered Hairball at the camper. I pushed her again, "Who did you talk to?"

She gritted her teeth to stay calm, and, I felt, to refrain from killing me to shut me up. "I have a private life, Norby. Leave me alone." She was sad for doing what she was doing, but had her own reason.

I reached over to touch her arm, and she let me. "Are we okay, Brew? Are we good?"

Her eyes were wet, but I knew I could still trust her. "Yeah, man, we're cool."

The Buick started and I turned on the heater. I looked up, and Brew had driven away. I looked around the interior of the car and felt Jeanine's presence everywhere. She was far from being a girly-girl, but she was still a girl. The trappings of a strong-willed young woman who had devoted her life to the business we had both built.

I drove out to get Hairball and reload my Sig. The cat had crapped on the camper floor, and made a puddle to go with it. I tossed a towel on top of the mess. I did my own relief thing in the weeds and climbed back into the Buick. Hairball found his own spot on my lap.

I ran my fingers through the thick dark gray fur covering my new friend. Do people give cats a bath? I might try. The animal was dirty and needed something. Food? A female cat? I didn't know any more about cats than I did about women. This was Rikki's cat, and I shouldn't get too attached. He lay in my lap, his engine purring while he clawed my legs in a totally content mood.

Rikki! I had to find her.

CHAPTER
TWENTY-NINE

● ●

THE BUICK GOT ME TO THE SHIP YARD where it was obvious something unusual had happened. At the far end there was a group of squad cars sitting at odd angles, the bright blue-and-red lights flashing in a disarrayed tangle. It was apparent to me what the fuss was about, but then, it could be a pinochle game, or free coffee and doughnuts. My first inclination was to rush down there and start screaming for Rikki, but my gut told me different.

At some point I needed to find out what went down last night. Did they make a bust and free a bunch of girls? Is the country safe from sex traffickers? Maybe on the first thought, but I knew better on the latter.

I slowly threaded the Buick through the maze of corrugated metal warehouses and was surprised at the lack of traffic at this end. Buried in worry and doubt if I was sniffing at the wrong end of the dock, I was suddenly jolted back to reality. The oxidized light-blue tail end of Brew's Cavalier was sticking out from the corner of a warehouse. I had missed it on my first go around. I parked out of sight and watched.

I was close, I could feel it.

Stroking Hairball, I swore at myself for wasting time. That tingling sensation was starting to get active again, and I became scared. What was Brew doing here, at this particular spot, right now? I battled my need to trust her against my inclination to put a bullet through her head. Her last word to me was about her going to the hospital this morning. Something was more important, and the call she made last night had guided her here.

I told Hairball, "Wait here, and don't crap on anything." I pressed the door shut so it wouldn't make any noise, and crept up behind the Cavalier. Moving to the front I felt the hood. Cold. She had come here straight from the Fields house. She got rid of me and came here.

My Sig led me to a partially open door in the building where she was parked. Made sense. In spite of my beer gut, I slid in the door opening, fully aware that it could be a trap. I didn't care. The whole building was dark and damp. Puddles of stagnant water sat here and there, and the dripping to add to them echoed against the tin sides.

There was a commotion someplace inside. The echoing of voices in heated conversation. Anger. Listening as close as my good ear would allow, I figured them to be coming from above me. Stairs. There had to be stairs in here, someplace. Shuffling around the perimeter, I saw the metal steps and handrail up ahead. Looking up, I saw zilch. I didn't own a pair of expensive shoes, so most of what went on my feet were cheap tennie-runners. These were split on the sole and my socks were soaking up the stinky water. The Sig in the lead, I moved up the steps, testing each one. Not so much for safety, but because I didn't want to do this.

The top of the steps ended at a mezzanine with no guard rail on it. I looked down and pictured me racing myself to the floor, head first, like a bug to a windshield. Shit.

The voices had quit. No, there they are again. Where? Oh, shit, where? Yelling, swearing, two voices—women's. Crap from dead ancient industry was strewn on the grated metal flooring; cardboard, old pallets, just crap. There was an aisle between pallet racking leading to another mezzanine, and I followed it to the yelling. If they were trying to hide, they were doing a shitty job of it. They were angry enough to not care about silence, and that was working in my favor.

A broken skylight over the other mezzanine lit up where they were. Creeping way too slowly, I had an urge to bust out and run pell-mell into whatever was out there. I had no argument that I was not the smartest dude, but I wasn't the dumbest either. The biggest convincer to do this slowly was fear.

Up ahead, real close.

Then I saw them. Both of them, and my fear turned into anger. My mind exploded and took control. I would never be able to explain why I screamed as I ran, but it bolted out of my mouth. Both women, stunned, turned to my stupid act and proved once again that girls are smarter than guys. Me, anyway.

I knew I was raising the Sig to fire, but it all came to a screeching halt before my finger could compose a decent squeeze on the trigger. The sole of a woman's tennis shoe met my face and crushed it. My head snapped back, and I felt it hit the metal floor with a ringing sound.

Through bell ringing between my ears, and the haze that clouded my eyes, I saw Rikki. White, standing alone, arms stretched up, her mouth a perfect circle as she was yelling at me. There was no sound, other than the freight train that was racing through my head. No whistle, just the thundering roar as I thought forty tons of steel were rolling over me. Then, I thought I was dying as everything turned a sickly gray-white, and became fuzz. If this is death, it's grossly over rated.

The voices again, louder, screaming.

Much to my disappointment, I started becoming conscious again. Oh, man, that hurt. My legs moved, a little, and my fingers moved, but they were surprisingly light and empty. The Sig was not where I wanted it to be.

Moaning was useless, but it was all I had. I forced my body to become upright, and had to turn to the side to do it. In my unconscious state I had evidently barfed all over myself, and the slime rolled down to the floor, dripping through the metal grating. Up on one elbow, I looked right into the dull blue eyes of my friend Bruin Heinz. The blood pouring from the slit in her neck had coated the grating under me. As I tried to navigate into an upright position, the slime was very hard to overcome. If I didn't, I knew that my blood would be added to hers. As unsteady as a newborn, I wavered on my feet, my arms hanging uselessly at my side. I looked up and muttered, "Hi, Kathleen. Long time no see."

"Mr. Klein, you have no idea of all the work I had to do just to get another date with you. You're playing hard to get, you naughty boy." She stood defiantly in front of me, grinning, in control, getting ready to finish her plan.

Though my head felt like Quasimoto was swinging on his bell clapper inside, I was gaining my composure, "Kathleen, you look like shit. You need to eat more than semen." The darkness glazed over her eyes, but she stayed in place. I was trying to get her to come to me and away from Rikki. Rikki, strung up by the hands, her feet barely touching the cold metal floor. Rikki, totally naked, her beautiful young body laced with streaks of blood, bruises, and fresh cuts. All Rikki could do, other than choke on her tears, was a muffled cry because Kathleen was standing in front of her, holding my Sig, pushed way too far into Rikki's mouth. I saw the hammer had been cocked back.

I wheezed, hoping I had enough strength to be loud enough to be heard, "You want me, you sadistic bitch. Leave her alone, she's just a kid. You and me, Kathleen. One more roll in the satin sheets before you waste me. Wouldn't it be sweeter to watch me bleed some more? I've got a little left."

I moved towards her and slipped in Brew's blood that had started to coagulate on the grating at my feet. I yelled, "Shit," and went down. Now, I knew it was providence that made me fall. I landed on Brew's back, my hands landing on the leather pouch strapped to her belt in back. The small holster the held the Beretta. I made a show of struggling to my knees while I jacked a slug into the chamber. My back to psycho bitch, I stood and spun around with the Berretta pointed at her face.

This of course made her laugh. "Why you stupid old fart. You think that pea shooter is going to stop me, honey bunch? You could hold a flame thrower to me and I wouldn't give a damn." Her voice rose, echoing through the building, and she laid her demented soul out before me. "I was born and bred to do things like this. I'm the poster child for fucked up families."

Her agitation scared me, and the tears rolling down her cheeks told me she was at the end of the game.

She screeched, "My mother? What a piece of ice she was. She watched my father, my own father, have sex with me. He got me pregnant and they didn't want a bastard around their hallowed life. All I was ever good for was to get stoned and be a deposit for whatever dick my parents steered to me. You are oh so right, you miserable piece of crap, I'm sick. My mind is twisted and I don't care anymore, that's why I can do what I want."

She was shaking and crying, and I could have moved at the speed of light and never be fast enough for what she did next. She screamed, "I DON'T GIVE A SHIT." The hammer on my Sig let go and Rikki's head split into tiny pieces. Before the first bit hit the wall behind, I had emptied the .22 into the face and body of the demented woman. She was crazed to the point of not knowing she had been shot five times.

Her face was a globe of hamburger, her body bleeding, and she charged me. I had been through this before, and had nightmares of her doing it again, so I was prepared. As her foot came lunging at me with the speed of a diving eagle, I moved to the left and grabbed it. The momentum pushed me down. On the floor with her standing over me, she raised the other foot to cave in my head.

I twisted the leg I had in my grasp and she went down. She grunted, "Uhn." On my knees, I held on tightly, slamming her shin against my knee. She screamed and I felt the resistance break as I snapped her fibula. I stood, holding what felt like a rubber band, and tried to tear it from her body.

Her anger overtook the pain and she lay on the floor writhing and screaming obscenities at me. This had to be the end. Only one, or neither of us, would live to see tomorrow. My brain was on a rocket ship going to hell. I stood on Hell's doorstep and will drag her with to put a stop to the madness.

I dropped onto her chest with my knee, crushing a shit load of ribs. Man, that felt good. Convinced she wasn't going anywhere, I went to the horrible hanging remains of my sweet little girl. I cut her down and laid her gently on the floor, apologizing for the dirt and cold. I couldn't look at her face. There was no life left in it. What remained was nothing more than the shell that once held the bubbly, innocent young girl.

I had something else to do. I turned back to Kathleen, on the floor. She had gotten hold of Brew's Beretta and was holding it to her own head, uselessly clicking the trigger on the empty chamber. I sat on her chest, grinding the broken bones into whatever organs they could find.

Kathleen was panting, breathlessly preaching, "Kill me. Please. This hurts so much. You bastard. You ruined us."

I pried the weapon from her fingers and slipped it into my pocket. She was mine now and I wasn't done. "You shouldn't have killed her, Kathleen. She had no reason to die. And, I have no reason to show you mercy."

I had things to do and wasn't going to let her crawl to the edge of the mezzanine. If she was going to die it had to be my hands that do it. I stood on her knee and snapped her other leg up. She felt the pain and the fear that intensified it.

Crude and cruel, as far as anyone was concerned, I was sure. To me, it wasn't enough.

I stepped to Brew and closed her eyes.

About two hours later, I had both Rikki and Brew outside, covered with old tarps, lying across the hood of the Cavalier.

I went back upstairs and stood over Kathleen watching the blood boil from her lips. I picked up the Sig from the floor and started the final phase. The slide was covered with the Remains of Rikki, so I used my bloody shirt tail to wipe it clean.

I knelt next to her head brushing the hair out of her eyes. Her chest was heaving, giving her short spasmodic breaths. I wanted to prolong the pain she was in, but thought I needed to speed this up. When she died, I wanted it to be at my hands. "You were such a beautiful woman, Kathleen. And so terribly fucked up. You have to die, you know."

She rolled her eyes to me, and I thought of Jeanine lying on the ground. She managed, "Do it."

"I want it to hurt, Kathleen. I want the pain and fear to grind into you. I want you to take it all to hell with you. I'm going to kill you now."

This woman was a killing machine. Strong, vengeful, remorseless, she killed for pleasure. Her abilities to overcome any confrontation were legend. I've been beaten almost to death by her, and what I was about to do was ordained long ago. She looked at me and smiled, her lips whispering, "Thank you."

Her last act was to cause me as much grief as she could, and she chose killing Rikki to do it. Rikki had been kept alive this long just for this showdown. She had inflicted a pain into me that would never heal, and she was satisfied. She was in control up to the end. It was my job to kill her.

I put the muzzle of the Sig to her temple and watched her die, knowing it would haunt me to my dying day. Yet, I was satisfied.

I called Frank Tellworth and told him where Rikki and Brew were and where to find Kathleen. I asked about the operation and he confirmed that the entire gang had been eliminated, Burton Fields brother, Gordon, was behind bars, and thirty girls were in a shelter, waiting to be sent home. I congratulated him. He told me he'd take care of the mess I made at the warehouse. He thought he owed it to us.

I spent the next two weeks waiting for Jeanine in the hospital.

CHAPTER
THIRTY

● ●

I HAD BEEN CAMPED OUT IN THE HOSPITAL waiting room so long I thought about bringing in my Lazy-Boy and TV set. The staff, well, most of them, were cordial but got tired of asking me if I wanted anything. Finally, a woman came in, cleared off the litter I had accumulated on the couch, and sat down. She was about as gorgeous as anyone in a hospital could get, and kept her professional aura between us. I wonder if she knew Dr. LaRioux.

"Mr. Klein, we need to talk. Your friend, Jeanine Forrester, is responding to us now and she's been asking for you. Evidently, just knowing you were here made her feel good. I'm going to arrange for you to be allowed permanent visitor status, as long as her signs remain stable. So, if you think you can behave yourself, I'll take you in to her."

All right, I'd been lectured. Now, I needed more information. "Who are you?"

"I'm Dr. Franken. I'll be monitoring her and scheduling her rehab. By the way, I understand the two of you were business partners. We can't find any insurance information for her. Was there a health plan through whatever business you two had?"

Business, of course. This place didn't run itself on charity. "I'll take care of that. Tell me what the future holds for her. Can she walk? Will she be able to move on her own? Will she ever make love again?"

Dr. Franken apparently had no sense of humor. "What?"

"Never mind that. What's she going to be facing?"

"There's not much hope for her being very mobile. A lot has been damaged, but with the proper care she'll make great strides. That brings me back to what I was asking before you interrupted me. So far we're treating her on a temporary status. We haven't been informed of any insurance."

"In other words, who's going to pay for all this."

"Uh huh, precisely."

"I will. Give her what she needs."

"Excuse me, Mr. Klein, but you don't appear to be in any position to . . ."

"Don't be judgmental, Dr. Franken. I'll take care of it." I stood, "Now, let's get me to her, shall we."

Dr. Franken was not the first person I'd pissed off, and wouldn't be the last. I followed her well-rounded rear through a maze of hallways, to a room filled with windows on the aisle side. Stopping outside, I started to get sick. *Don't do anything stupid, Klein.* A little late for me to think of that.

She was lying flat in a bed with guard rails to keep her from running away. Tubes and wires were sprouting from everywhere. The beeping and humming was almost musical, but after a few minutes I'd probably rip it all out. But, that's just me.

The most glorious thing I've seen for a long time came in the shape of a wide smile. "Hi, Norbs. I was told you were here sleeping in a dumpster." Her voice was small and raspy.

"Yeah, I found the one they toss all the old parts into. Man, you should see some of the stuff people give up in here."

Threading my way between the tubes and wires, I leaned in and kissed her. Her lips were dry and cracked. I reached over for the ice water and gave her a slug. "Before long I can give you a beer. With a bendy straw."

"I'd like that."

The good Dr. Franken interrupted, "I'm going to leave you alone now. Mr. Klein, don't become a nuisance." And with that gentle refrain, she left us alone.

Jeanine was laughing, "Your reputation precedes you."

I pulled a chair up and sat holding her hand. God, she felt good.

"The police were here. I told them as much as I could."

I couldn't add to that, the cops knew all they needed to know.

She asked, "What happened, Norbs? I mean after. The police wouldn't tell me anything. They mentioned something about the feds stonewalling them. You have anything to do with that?"

"Yeah, I do. There's a lot for us to talk about, honey, but it'll wait until later. Today is just a I'm-so-frigging-glad-to-be-with-you day."

"I think I'm a charity case here and don't know how much longer I'll be able to call this home."

"Got it covered, babe. You'll get everything you need. I sold my Plymouth and set up an account for you. You're rich."

She knew how ludicrous that was, but didn't push it. She knew, and she knew that I knew she knew. Can you follow that?

We talked the rest of the day, and I carefully covered the mayhem in the warehouse. I guided her through her grief for Brew and Rikki and called the duty nurse for a sedative. She was terribly upset over what took place, but understood the reality of why.

Late in the afternoon, when the magic of pharmaceutical miracles overwhelmed her and she fell asleep, I slipped out. I had something to do and didn't want to be late. I opened the trunk of the Plymouth and tugged the fiber panel out that lined the inside of the trunk. Reaching in I pulled out a large plastic envelope, and went to the bank.

The banker stared at the stack of bearer bonds and couldn't close his mouth. He looked at me and uttered, "What?"

"Yeah, I know, it's a lot. I want to set up an account in the name of Jeanine Forrester. It's to be a annuity that pays out dividends to her for life. When hospital bills start coming in I want them paid. I'll have my name on it, but when I die the account will be hers alone."

We hammered out some details, made it all legal and tax free, and I left, feeling pretty damn good.

The next morning came way too soon. I got up and let Mrs. Feldstein dress me. I accepted her coffee, but was in no mood for anything else. No booze in the coffee. I needed to be sober for this. I had a funeral to go to.

Police funerals were the same as military funerals. All the rigid formality of respect to the departed, along with the rifle salute and presentation of the flag. Rikki would have loved this if she had been on our side of it. They were all here for her. They respected her and they loved her. They knew she was a good cop, and that would have made her happy. That was what she wanted.

Squad cars flooded the cemetery, lined up for miles in the narrow asphalt lanes. Officers taking their own time off to drive all the way from Minneapolis, and as far as Chicago. The governor was there, and a slew of mayors and police chiefs. I saw Stu Grosslein across the way, but kept the distance between us. My job, now, was to keep Sy Thielges from collapsing. He kept his promise to not drink before it was over. Brian Melland stood on the other side of me. We were all crying.

Words were spoken, eulogies were portioned out, and then those damn bagpipes started wailing. I had nothing against bagpipes. I was glad they were here playing the traditional "Amazing Grace." It's just that the sound cut through me like a sword, tearing out anything that I held dear.

Rikki was being honored.

The seven rifles were pointed up. A lone solitary voice gave the command, "One . . . two . . . three." I wanted to die. We all stood, wavering in grief, while the flag was folded. A tall police officer, dressed splendidly in his uniform, stepped to Sy, gently handing it to him. Over Sy's wailing, I heard the officer say, "God bless you and your daughter. If there is anything you ever need, I'll be there for you." Generic, but I knew it was a genuine gesture.

Sy stood numbly waiting for me to finish my business with Frank Tellworth. Brian waited with him.

Out of anyone's earshot, I was told, "I wanted to make sure you and I were okay with each other. There are some loose ends you need to know about so you don't fulfill your promise to kill me." His grin was not appreciated.

I asked, "Did you take Brew's body?"

"Yes, I did. You need to understand that Bruin Heinz was one of our operatives. She was working with a few outside sources, as well as our inside plant. She was actually an undercover CIA agent. I told you we had been on this for over seven years."

I was getting sick.

He got on to what I really needed to know. "Officer Thielges was the most important element of this whole operation. She volunteered to become a sex toy for the gang in the Fields house."

I winced.

He reached out and gave me a friendly arm squeeze. That wasn't going to keep me from puking on him.

"I know this is going to be hard for you to digest, and I would avoid telling her father any of this. They were rough with her, and she had no delusions as to what she was to them. She was one of the strongest women I've ever worked with, and the information she passed made the bust possible."

He reached into his pocket and withdrew the key ring to Rikki's GT 390 Mustang.

They felt strange and heavy in my hand. "She gave me specific instructions to be sure that you got this if anything ever happened to her. Somehow, I think she knew where she was headed."

My head was swirling, and I choked down the bile fighting to burst through my face. Oh, dear God, no.

I had one last question, "Your plant, in the Fields house. They get out?"

His answer was slow, but I didn't want to hear anymore than what he volunteered. "Yes, they got out and are reassigned. That's all I can tell you on that."

I was sincere, "Good for them." How was I going to get through this now? Tellworth nodded and walked away.

Shuffling across the grass, I held tightly to Sy, pulling Brian with us. I wasn't done with him. Sy turned down the offer by the funeral director for a ride home. Clutching the flag, he climbed into the Reliant, and I shut the door. Brian's car was two behind us.

I told him, "Brian, she was very fond of you, and you were probably the first guy she would consider loving." I reached in my pocket and pulled out a tiny Saran wrapped item and handed it to him. "She kept this in her jewelry box because you gave it to her." I handed the green M&M to him, hugged him tightly, and left him standing in his grief.

Stopping in front of his house, Sy assured me he wanted to be alone. I went to the hospital and told Jeanine about the whole affair.

She asked me, "What about Brew's body?"

All I could tell her, was, "I was going to get a plot in the cemetery where Laura was buried, but I got stonewalled when I asked about her body. It just disappeared. Kathleen was cremated and tossed in the garbage."

CHAPTER
THIRTY-ONE

JEANINE'S RECOVERY WAS LONG, ARDUOUS, AND FRUSTRATING. At first, depression guided her, and she gave up. She had an electric wheelchair. As long as she was on the first floor, she could move where she wanted. I bought her a van outfitted for stubborn people with mobility problems. It'd lift her up into the driver's seat and had hand controls. She was more than happy, but the tedium of doing basic movements got to her. There were many nights she would break down and cry her heart out. Then, she would swear at me, and I stood close so she could hit me. The next step was always to struggle up and fight to win. I mentioned a quote I heard once, that could be considered drippy, but she appreciated it, "Dying is easy. You have to fight to live."

I stayed by her side all the time. Once in a while I'd get a call for a job to follow a cheater and take their picture, just enough to keep me busy. Jeanine's turning point came late one night when she got a visit from Gloria Fields.

They sat and talked for hours, getting blitzed on wine and beer. An act totally out of Mrs. Fields's gallery, but she had something to prove to Jeanine, and took all night to do it. Jeanine went to bed and Gloria slept on the sofa. In the morning, she went into Jeanine's room and woke her up.

She tossed back the drapes and moved the wheelchair into a corner. Under protest, Jeanine barked, "What the hell are you doing? I need that chair."

The startling response, "Bullshit. You're just lazy. Get your ass out of bed and make me some coffee." She unfolded a seldom used walker and set it by the bed. "You want to sit in that damn chair the rest of your life? No, I won't let you."

Incredulous, Jeanine quipped, "What?"

"What, hell. I haven't got anything to do and I'm going nuts in that nursing home. I'm trying to get my mind off what happened back then, so I'm spending my time with you. You, my dear friend, are going to learn how to walk. Now, I asked for coffee. Go make it."

The two fought like polecats for a few days, until Jeanine discovered that she could actually walk behind the aluminum walker. I labeled it "Texas Ranger." You know, "Walker, Texas Ranger." Yeah, I know. Next, came a great celebration with the discard of the walker, and introduction of the cane.

In this story, that was as far as she got. I will say, though, that although it was years in the making, Jeanine became mobile again. She'd been active in the gym and has taken up with a physical therapist who owns the place. I think she's smitten. I checked him out and he looks like a genuine guy. I couldn't be happier for her.

Jeanine and I went to Hell Burger a few times, had some good food, good conversations, and good liquor. Brian Melland always sat and mixed conversation with us. He said he put the green M&M in a tiny glass box, in a special place.

One of the good things that happened, was finding the rifle that blew apart Angie's face, in the Fields house. It was processed, printed, and determined that Clete Michaels was not the shooter. After too long a stretch in the slammer, he was released. Today, he runs a ministry on the dumpy part of Superior Street, hopelessly trying to save a few souls. Hanky tried it once, but was afraid of someone finding out who he really was. The best part of Clete's work was counseling men who had some strange need to beat up women they loved. A few prison visits with good results got him a grant to expand his work. I was not much on the Jesus part of his program, but I went in to help once in a while. Whatever.

Two years went by since we busted the slave market on the Duluth waterfront. Sy Thielges was working hard at accepting what happened. We shared a few Nordeasts and hashed out the nostalgia from the past. All went well until his wife showed up one day. The one who left on Rikki's second day of life. She was broke and asked him to sell the house and give her the money.

I was there at the time. I sat on the broken cement steps watching Sy toss her out.

I tried counting the number of times she cart-wheeled down to the street. A lot. Her purse broke open in the fall, all her coke, pot, syringes, and pipe, flying every which way. Sy stormed out of the house, grabbed her by the collar, and marched her two blocks away, telling her he'd kill her if she showed up again. When he came back, out of breath, I handed him a beer and toasted his victory.

Two years.

Two years gone, and it wasn't over yet.

CHAPTER THIRTY-TWO

● ● ● ● ● ● ● ● ● ● ● ● ● ● ● ● ● ● ● ●

For a pad as expensive as this one, it would seem reasonable to expect it to be insulated from the elevator noise. It slammed to a stop, the doors opened, and I listened to Dr. Ariel LaRioux punch in the access code. She was alone, which made this a lot easier.

The fancy fish tank gave the room an eerie underwater greenish glow. Just enough illumination to let her know someone was sitting in her large, way too comfortable chair. Her startled comment, "What?" was followed by her turning on a normal light.

"Mr. Klein, what the hell do you think you're doing? How did you get in here?"

Man, she was pissed.

She moved at considerable speed to slam her hand on the emergency alarm connected to the security system. I held up a fuse, "It won't work. I need to put this back in."

Her being pissed went quickly into scared shitless mode. "How did you …?"

I stood up, "I'm a detective. I know how to do lots of sneaky things."

I watched her collect her amazing array of wits to take control of this situation.

She backed up to the bar and picked up a cut glass carafe of wine. Dribbling too much into a matching goblet, she became impolite. "I won't ask if you want some. I don't want you to stay."

"Gee, the last time I was here you couldn't find enough ways to fuck me. Now, you don't want me here? Very confusing, seeing as how I came with an answer to your last inquiry about the bonds."

The goblet of wine slipped from her incredibly long and soft fingers, bouncing on the plush beige carpet. Wine stains can be a bitch.

"But, you said . . ."

"Yeah, I know. It's tough on a relationship when we lie to each other."

Stepping closer to me than she should have, her interest in my being here changed. "So, you do have them." Running those incredible fingers across my cheek, she gave me that pouty little smile. "Well, what are we going to do about this news?"

I pushed her back, "What's this 'we' shit?"

"Oh, come now. It was only a matter of time before you realized how much I could do for you. Where, Norbert? Where are the nasty little things?"

"Ariel, you contemptuous little whore. I think you should learn where they were when you asked the first time."

Passing off the slur on her morality, she said, "Okay, let's play your game. Where, oh where, have the little bonds gone?" Her sing-song was cute in a disgusting way.

"In the trunk of my car. Hidden in plain sight. Who would-a thunk it?"

Now her face took on an ugly shape. "Your car? You can't be serious." She feigned a happy reaction, moving to the drawer in her desk. She opened it, gleaming at me with those intensely sexual eyes. "Now, isn't that just too much like you!" She coyly reached in the drawer, fumbling for what wasn't there. Her happy reaction turned quickly into panic.

I held up the dainty little Taurus .22 she was fumbling for. "It's not in there, Ariel."

I couldn't tell if she was angry or surprised. "How did you . . . ?"

"I'm getting tired of explaining to you, Ariel. I'm a detective and this is what ilk of my type do." I waved it in front of her. "Brew had one something like this, but in her hand, it would be far more deadly than in yours."

Stunned, she uttered, "Brew?"

"Yes, my dear. Bruin Heinz, your plant, your squeeze, your connection. Your lesbian liaison."

I stepped behind her, caressing her shoulder, then pulling the pin from the barrette that held her hair up. It cascaded down her back, and I ran my hand down the fine, soft, shiny, mane. Whispering through the strands, into her ear, "I put five of these tiny little bullets into Kathleen's face and body. Of course it didn't stop her. She was crazy, wasn't she. She didn't have a clue of right or wrong. You were counseling her on so many levels but never got through, did you? Then she got you to work on me for the bonds. I'm disappointed in your track record, Ariel. Nothing seems to be working for you."

The act was gone and she stiffened, listening to me unravel the whole story.

"When I put the final bullet into Kathleen's head I did what you were never able to do. I gave her eternal freedom. She's in hell for sure, but she was in hell here, on earth, as well. She's where she belongs. You know that, don't you!"

She started to turn, "No. Don't turn. Just sink to your knees."

"What?" Unbelieving, she was churning inside to decipher my words.

"Like when you gave me that incredible fifteen minutes of oral sex. Remember? Just like then, on your knees, and you don't even have to get naked."

Whatever compels someone to satisfy a terrorist's commands is a mystery to me. Trembling, she was searching for the key to get away from this, yet complied hoping that I would be happy with her and leave. She sank to the carpet, her hands hanging still at the ends of her dangling arms. Taking a moment to straighten her skirt, she seemed to be ready. Ready for what? Redemption? Freedom? The bonds? My going away?

She came to the moment of realization when I pressed the bore of the small gun to the back of her head. She didn't struggle to get up, run away, scream, or plead. She just gave up and bawled.

The real pain is in the agony of waiting for the inevitable. The bullet was fast and instantly destructive. She knelt in place for a brief moment, then fell forward, the bloody front of her head spoiling the carpet even more than the wine.

I wiped everything clean and gave the gun back to her.

CHAPTER
THIRTY-THREE

• •

I REALLY DIDN'T LIKE DRIVING THE MUSTANG, harboring a deep feeling of guilt. Sy insisted that he never wanted to see the car again and I was more than welcome to it. I still held on to my classic Plymouth Reliant. Anyone could always use a spare car. Every time I sat in the Mustang I got a pang in my heart that drove me crazy. And what a short trip that was. I struggled with my decision for a long time and finally decided if I didn't do it, I'd never get the nerve.

Making a reservation at Hell Burger was really not necessary. If there were no empty tables out front, I'd sit in the kitchen. Tonight, I called and requested that Brian Melland be my host for the night. I gave Mitch a fifty-dollar bill to cover Brian's wages for the time I was there, and he became my guest. I bought him dinner and got him drunk.

We both steered clear of the Rikki part of the conversation, but it hung over us like a heavy fog, ready to choke us. Brian would be a son to me for the rest of my life. We had shared and lost something that cannot be replaced. Brian was beginning to sing Irish ballads, so I knew he was done eating and beginning to drink. The only way he could cover the loss we shared was to get drunk and sign loudly. I sang awhile, but then it was time to go. I paid for the meal and gave Brian his tip.

I laid the title to the Mustang on the table, the keys on top, kissed him and left.

• •

ONE REALLY COOL THING ABOUT BEING A PRIVATE detective is the ability to sneak up and spy on people, then gather information to make their life unbearable. Nobody has ever been anxious to do surveillance. It can be a long drawn-out fruitless affair that gives you nothing but a sore butt, and a need to pee too much coffee. Staying unnoticed is the key to success, so too much, or even any, movement can blow a lot of time wasted on being a snoop.

I probably hated doing this more than anyone. Yet, my mission was one that made me relish every moment. The Reliant was a perfect stake out vehicle, because none of the interior lights worked, and only some of the dash lights. I could get out, stretch, take that pee, and get some fresh air. A good way to get rid of time.

Like a few others, I've resorted to listening to audio books, or music, on head phones to pass the time. On this gig, I was adamant about not missing a single thread. I picked up my target and followed at the recommended distance, plus an insurance of a little more space between us. The car they were using was really hard to loose.

I did my work over a period of a couple weeks, taking my time to be certain everything fell into place. The routine was always the same. So predictable. And in this case, so dangerous—for them. I backed off, waited another week doing nothing, then went back at it. Bingo, the same stupid routine.

The toys in my war chest were getting sparse, with only a few of the choice ones left. And, one special gadget I was saving just for this purpose. The nice thing about the Colt.357 Magnum was that it could do so much more than it was intended for. To me, in what I was about to delve into, the slug would stop a black bear, more than enough. At close range, not something to talk about.

The particular piece I was looking at was picked up by me a very long time ago, thinking I needed to stop somebody from doing an evil deed to me. Thankfully, I never had to use it. There was no serial number, and it was clean of any prints. I put on a pair of Nylon gloves and handled the piece very carefully. Reverently, really.

About 2:00 a.m., as dark as it would ever get, and it was time to start playing for real. I picked up the target the same as always, trailing behind it. First, a stop at Dunkin' Dounuts, taking time to flirt with the girl behind the counter, then a swing through the downtown section to log miles. On schedule, the next stop was a remote parking lot up on the hill above Duluth, taking its special spot in a far corner.

This routine was so utterly ridiculous, but knowing the character of the car's driver, it all made sense. Firstly, the unmistakable white color, with the streamers and emblems festooned on the sides were a sore thumb. Next, the chrome adorning the roof and the lights attached, it looked like a circus wagon. Send in the clowns.

A police car is intended to be seen, so hiding in one doesn't make much sense. The next item doesn't happen every night, but tonight was special. I knew the hooker who went by the name of Froosie. I had no idea why such a name was appealing, but, what the hey. The confines in a police car were crowded because of all the gadgets inside. She stripped her top off, adjusted her hoo-hoos, and climbed in the passenger side. The driver went through the actions required to pull his pants down, Froosie's head went into his lap, and budda-bing.

It only took a few minutes. He handed her the fee, and she took off, putting her shirt back on while she walked. Her stiletto heels sounded like castanets on the asphalt.

All quiet now and time to play the game. The driver had lit a cigarette before taking time to pull his pants up. Perfect. I sidled up to the window and scared the shit out of him, "Hello, Snerd, working hard?"

He jumped so high his head hit the roof. "Jesus."

Collecting his nervous system, he glared at me, "Klein, what the fuck are you doing. I oughta run you in. Don't ever do that to a guy. Shit." He made an attempt to hide his bare legs.

"Sorry, Snerd, I just wanted to extend the gratitude of the tax payers of Duluth for keeping them safe tonight. And all the other nights."

"Fuck you, Klein. What do you want? Get out of here."

I let a moment pass before I leveled on him. "You were the snitch in the department, Snerd. You worked with Bruin Heinz a long time ago, and connected in our case to help her."

That turned him cold. "Huh? What are you talking about?"

"You were feeding the sex traffic gang all the data to keep them alerted on what we were doing. A snitch."

"That was two years ago."

"Doesn't matter. Officer Thielges is still dead. You helped do that."

He actually had the balls to grin. "Thielges, oh yeah. We all got to sample that. Sweet stuff."

Now my blood was percolating into the top of my head, like an old coffee pot. When he felt the muzzle of the .357 press against his temple, the grin faded. "What . . . What are you doing?"

"Exacting revenge. Does that confuse you?"

He started to scramble, looking for a way out of this. Before he had a chance to hit the radio, I told him, "You made a fatal mistake, Snerd. You helped kill her. Rot in hell with Kathleen Pierpont and the shrink." The blast, while somewhat muffled by his skull and the interior of the vehicle, was deafening. Space occupied where his head used to be, the matter splayed over the shattered passenger window, dripping little chunks of red and pink stuff in a pretty psychedelic pattern.

I tossed the gun into the car, turned, and walked away.

I should feel some regret for doing this, but I can't find it. I owe a lot of people a lot of things, and will always be regarded as a dead-beat, but these are debts I will pay, no matter what the cost.

Rikki was gone and I needed to compensate for that. I didn't care if it was wrong.

CHAPTER
THIRTY-FOUR

● ●

I SAT IN STU'S OFFICE, WAITING. My status as a volunteer-cop-wanna-be-consultant had been revoked. I was just Norby Klein, plain old citizen. I was afforded the pleasure of a free cup of diarrhea coffee, when there was some. And there usually was, because not too many in the precinct were desperate enough to drink it. Also, there was a rumor of some kind of health issue.

Stu had his lunch jammed in a drawer, the brown paper sack crumpled to fit all the way in. I pulled it out and was greeted with the magical odor of a peanut butter and Miracle Whip sandwich. Man, I loved those things. I didn't want to be a hog, so I ate the whole thing. Maybe he'd never miss it.

I had the bag shoved back in place before he came storming in. He bellowed, "Klein, what the hell do you want? Get out."

He really did love me.

"Hi, Stu-man. Just hanging around, pretending to be appreciated."

"Well, that ain't going to happen here."

He lit a cigarette, not department policy, absently tossing the match in my cup.

"You seem upset, Stu. What's shakin' besides the flap of flesh under your jaw?" My insult went over his head. I was sitting in his chair and made no move to give it back to him. He stomped around the office, finally hoisting his blubby body up on the credenza. I wanted to get him in a good mood, asking, "You going to run for city council again? Maybe this time you'll get some votes."

His mood just got darker. "Shut up, asshole. I got some votes. Almost a hundred."

He looked at me and realized I was in his chair and he was sitting on the furniture. He slid down, snarling, "Go on, get out of my chair."

I obeyed and started to brighten his day by pretending to leave. Darkening it again, I turned and asked, "Say, Stu, you want to go fishing? We can take the Winnebago up to Hovland and get us some of them twenty-pounders."

He considered it, but declined. "Naw, I better stick around. The chief is still on the warpath about Snerds being snuffed. Nobody can figure it out, but then, nobody liked him."

"Suit yourself, buddy. I'm going and I know of no better way to get rid of unwanted baggage than sitting in a boat with a beer, listening to the Twins lose a game."

He pushed back in his squeaky chair, the magic of reminiscence brightening his face. Smiling, he brought back some happy times. "Remember when we caught those lake trout? Do you think that lady in the restaurant would cook them for us again? That was so good."

"You mean Lisa, at the Chicago Bay Marketplace? I know she would. Her special shore-line breading and homemade tartar sauce. Nothing better. She's put in a liquor store now. We can go power shopping."

The nostalgia swept over him and put him in a day dream trance. "You know, that really is a good idea." He turned and looked out the dirty window, "I need a rest, Norby. I need to get away. Things aren't going well with Noreen, and some time away might be good. For both of us."

He turned back to me with the look of a kid in a toy store at Christmas. "When are you going?"

"Sooner the better, but I'll wait until you're ready. I can take some time to clean up the motor home and fix a bit on the boat."

He wrung his hands in anticipation, and then turned dark. "You think the weather will be good? You know I hate the water. I never learned to swim, you know."

I clapped him on the hammy part of his shoulder, and said, "Yeah, I know you can't swim, and I heard the weather will be decent for a couple weeks."

Excited, he stammered, "Weekend after next, okay? I have to clean up a few things and get the chief off my back."

The opaque glass door rattled when I shut it behind me. I paused staring at the empty desk where Rikki once ruled the office. Oh, shit, it was coming back. I better get out of here. Outside, I stumbled to the Plymouth, got in, then waited until the shaking stopped.

Rikki.

• •

THE WINNEBAGO WAS STILL AS BEAUTIFUL AS EVER, in all of its oxidized glory. I tossed a set of new used tires on it and finally patched the awning leak with duct tape. Hairball sniffed the spot I cleaned from his dump last time he was in it. I suppose the spot is his now. Fine, I'll use the toilet.

The fourteen-foot Lund aluminum fishing boat was a wee bit old, but still as good as new. A few dents and scratches just added charm. These babies were built to last. I had a few modifications to make, made sure the trailer had current tabs, and the brake lights worked. I piled in everything that would be needed, and a few extras.

The Winnie was filled with gas, the propane was tight, and all the tires were round. A cooler filled with ice and beer, a quart of Jack Daniels, frozen pizza in the freezer, and it was ready.

On the day of departure I hooked up the trailer and took off to pick up Stu at his house. Armed with a cup of coffee, I sat in front of his house honking the horn. At last, he came bounding out, Isabelle close behind. Oh, shit, no. Was she going to ask to go with? She couldn't, not this time.

Stu was dressed like a Ron Schara clone, without the dog. He must have gone wild in Cabela's. A few of the tags were still attached, but I left it alone. The comic value was worth his embarrassment. Isabelle kissed him goodbye, and said to me, "Have a good time, Mr. Klein. See ya."

I absorbed this moment, wishing I had a daughter to kiss me goodbye. I shook it off, accepting my lot in life. Rikki, again. I wondered if it would ever be good again.

The drive up Highway 61, skirting the shore of Lake Superior, was beyond pleasant. We had a beer or two, listened to some oldies radio station, and traded lies about the past. Stu was in a good mood. He reached into his camo-colored vest, fumbled a moment, the drew out a couple of huge cigars.

"I was going to save these for the campfire, but I feel this is a special moment."

He handed one to me, punched the cigarette lighter, stoked the weed, and became buried in a cloud of smoke. I followed suit, and one would think we had a fire in here with the smoke we generated. A usual stop in Silver Bay for hamburgers at the Northwoods café topped off a great day so far. The fries, as usual, were to die for.

The singing died down by the time we cruised through Grand Marais, and just chatted from there up to Hovland. I parked the Winnie near the old concrete pier, level enough to do the job. This wasn't a typical camping spot, but it worked out just fine. Once in a while, a curious homebody would wander by to say, "Hello." Just nice folks, being nice.

We farted around the rest of the day, got hammered, and told more lies. Late at night we played a few games of Skip-Bo, and the dice game ten-thousand. I had a reason to let Stu clean my slate, and he gloated in triumph. I was happy to oblige him.

The next morning, good coffee and hash browns with scrambled eggs and sausage. Man. I stalled going on the lake, looking for the perfect time. About five that afternoon I saw it on the horizon. A dark bank of clouds, which I didn't mention.

Stu was poking into the fire with a stick, having fun with the sparks. "Stu, let's mount the horses and do some fishing."

He jumped up too fast, getting a dizzy spell. I had the boat loaded, the beer in a cooler, and the minnow bucket under the middle seat. I directed a very nervous man into the bow seat, and took my place at the stern. I cranked on the Evinrude, and got a cough and spurt of exhaust on the first pull. Four more pulls and we were running.

I could tell Stu was nervous, and tried to avoid the bigger waves. The cloud bank from the north was getting bigger, and I steered into it so he couldn't see what was up ahead. The wind was picking up, and it was getting colder.

The shoreline was barely visible, with our spot well to the south of where we were now. Then, it happened—the Evinrude died. I took it calmly, because I knew it would. It took a moment for Stu to realize we were just bobbing, no motor sound.

"Hey, what happened? We gonna fish here?"

"It's too deep to fish here, Stu."

"Well, let's get going."

"Can't Stu, we're out of gas."

"What? What do you mean. You had everything all set up. Start the damn motor."

He looked around and saw nothing. I looked at him and saw fear.

"Stu, there's no gas."

"Oars! We can row back."

"Sorry, Stu, I forgot the oars."

Now was the time for fear to ignite panic. "Klein, what have you done? I don't like this." Then he noticed something he should have seen back at the pier. "Where are the life jackets?"

"Forgot them also, Stu."

His yelling had a muted cast to it, going no place in the density of the lake. The waves were picking up and a mist started. "Klein, do something."

"I am, Stu. I'm about to do something." I reached into my pocket, "I have something of yours, Stu. Unfortunately, the battery is dead and there's no signal anyway." I handed his cell phone to him, stepping along the boat to the bow, making a show of wobbling against the increasing waves.

He grabbed the gunwales and pressed his feet to the bottom, then took the phone and got a stupid look on his face. "Where?"

"At your house, when you were burning hamburgers for your fans. Isabelle gave it to me. You know, Stu, that in this day and age, communication is a shared element. When I used your phone to call Jeanine, when I saw the kid dead in my car, I saw your calls-made log."

Screaming at me, "Yeah, so what? We're gonna sink out here." He was going into a higher level of panic, so I needed to move this up.

"You are the one who called Clark Desmond in the surveillance van the night Rikki disappeared. You were the inside contact that was feeding the traffickers and Kathleen Pierpont with the information. You blindsided us, and ultimately, you and Snerd were responsible for Rikki's death."

Stu and I had been friends for life and had shared a lot of moments. This particular moment was going to be close and personal. He sat stunned, holding the little useless device, his jowls shaking from fright and the impending revelation of something he thought he had been insulated from. He blubbered, "Oh, God, you know?"

"Yeah, Stu, I know. I put the whole thing together and am tightening the loose ends. I think Tellworth is a little deeper than he wants me to know, but that's something I'll have to work on."

I didn't take time to ask the burning question why. It didn't matter now. I took out Brew's little .22 that I shot Kathleen with. I handed it to him. "There's one bullet, Stu. You can kill me, or put one in your brain to avoid what I am going to do to you." He was shaking like an elm tree in a tornado, and when he pulled the trigger, the bullet sailed off into the water. He missed me by a mile.

I leaned over his legs, took the anchor cord, and wrapped it around his ankles. I stood up and violently rocked the boat back and forth. It was raining hard now, and freezing cold.

He sat dumbfounded, the rain dripping down his face, the sparse growth of hair clinging to his forehead, the cell phone in one hand, the useless pistol in the other. He dropped them to clamp his hands to the gunwales until they turned white. He stared at me wondering if I was trying to scare him, or do something unwanted.

Both.

His nervous system woke up and he got pissed. About time.

Yelling insanely about fairness, a bitch of a wife, me, and how he was never appreciated. I could have given him the specifications on that one. His quaking voice was lost in the wind.

My feet were planted to the sides and I started rocking again. Back and forth, each swing brought the gunwales closer to the water level.

Time to open the toy box and let the real surprises out. True confession time. And, one lie to make him suffer more. "The night of your candidate's party? When Noreen got blitzed? We screwed in the basement, Stu. I made love to your wife. How does that make you feel?"

He rose from the seat forgetting his fear of what was happening right now. "You dirty bastard. How could you?" He attempted a pathetic lunge at me, but I rocked a little more and he collapsed back where he belonged, his frozen hands clinging to the aluminum rails.

Now, for some true stories. The wind was getting too strong, whipping us with a major storm, so I had to yell. "The bonds, Stu. The bonds. Everyone wanted the bonds. Want to know where they are? Millions in redeemable bonds? Want to know, Stu?"

He stared at me, his lips blue around the gaping mouth, unbelieving.

"Laura has them. I put them in her casket when she was buried. You can go get them if you want. I have no use for them. The rest were in the trunk of my piece of shit car. Oh, by the way, I blew the brains out of your partner, Snerd. It's payback for what was done to Rikki, Stu. I killed Kathleen, but you know that. I also did the shrink, with her own gun, no less. You and psycho-bitch got her involved to ply on my weakness for babes. I killed them all, Stu. Everyone. They were all implicated."

I was getting more pissed and thought about wringing his neck so I could look into his eyes at the moment of death. I also wondered if I should just give it up and let the poor bastard float out to sea. The vision of Rikki shot through my head, so I went on. Wailing through the tears, I screamed, "They were all so fucking smug thinking they could do what they wanted with the stupid washed up PI. Now, after you, I'm done and paid my debt."

On the brink of the unbelievable, he blubbered, "You're crazy. Stop this."

"Rikki, Stu. Think of her as you go down."

The boat, aided by the waves and wind, and my rocking, turned over, pulled in too much water, and went down. Tackle, beer cooler, empty gas can, all went crazy with no restrictions. Probably to join the *Edmund Fitzgerald*. I held Stu by the collar for a moment, keeping his face above the waves. "You forced my hand, Stu. You could have kept Rikki out of it. She was killed by a psychopathic monster for no other reason than to hurt me. Sorry, buddy, but you're going to die now. It won't be quick, and I apologize for that. Time for you to go to hell, Stu."

His arms flailed trying to grasp something. He tried to grab on to me, but I kept him at a distance and he couldn't. The anchor, tied to his ankles, was tugging on him. I let go of his collar and he looked at me, a pathetic begging man on the edge of a horrible death. I watched him sink from sight as he inhaled Lake Superior, filling his lungs with ballast. The top of his head was the last sight of my old friend.

I stripped off my outer jacket, letting it go. Yanking on the valve attached to the air canister on my life jacket, it inflated and I became buoyant. Kicking off my shoes, I paddled to shore, over a mile away.

CHAPTER
THIRTY-FIVE

●　●　●　●　●　●　●　●　●　●　●　●　●　●　●　●　●　●　●　●

I REALLY DIDN'T EXPECT TO REACH SHORE, and I didn't care. I did what I was compelled to do, and that felt good. I was dragged a little too far south and landed near the Naniboujou Lodge. I lay on the shore being rolled back and forth by the waves, toying with me, like a cat with a mouse. I was conscious of what was going on, but spun in and out of reality. I was being tossed around inside of a mental time warp listening to Kathleen yelling, "I don't give a shit." I didn't either. Kill me, go ahead. By now, that would be the most redeeming thing. I thought I had covered everything, thankful Jeanine would be taken care of. My biggest worry was Hairball locked up in the Winnie.

I was being dragged by the life vest, which had deflated, across the sand beach. My next recollection was sitting in the kitchen of the lodge sipping on a hot cup of brandy. Life. I had one stocking on, and was wrapped in a soft flannel blanket. People were hovering over me trying to be nice and get me stuff. I was shaking violently, but that had nothing to do with the cold. I had just murdered my best friend.

The highway patrolman sat in front of me taking notes on everything I said. I told him I thought our location, when the waves capsized us, was way to the north, and much closer to shore. Before the patrol car took me to Grand Marais for more questioning, the officer took me back to the Winnie to get changed, and pick up Hairball.

It took about six months before the incident was put to rest. I would never be able to go back to the precinct house again. Cops hold a bitter edge to their colleagues disappearing. With my reputation for being who I was, they just found another reason to hold a grudge. Fine.

I gave the Winnie to my friend, Bob Swearingen, who lived in Grand Marais. He took off in it and nobody has heard from him since. I have a hunch he wound up in Mexico with one of those enticing black-eyed beauties who could do the most wonderful things. I envy him.

I sit in the Hell Burger once in awhile talking to Pappy, Mitch, or Cynthia. They're my family, but I keep that to myself. Brian drives the Rikki-mobile on sunny Sundays, keeping it in storage when a drizzle threatens it. He's going to college, which is always good. However, I have a hunch he'll be with Mitch and Cyn for a very long time.

I called on Clete Michaels to check out his operation. I was highly surprised, and pleased, to be greeted by my friend Hanky. He's taken to the cure, for now, and is starting to talk to drunks who need a strong arm to hold on to. I think I'm a project for him.

Mrs. Feldstein keeps busy with her clutch of seniors and is going to move into the high-rise with them. Safe and always normal people to gossip and bitch with. I think there is an old guy who is enamored with her. She told him she'll have sex with him, but then he has to go.

Noreen paid off the mortgage with some of the incredible insurance Stu had. His retirement benefits will keep her in aces forever. She also discovered a stash of mysterious cash in the garage and is putting Isabelle through college. The same one Brian is going to. Hmm! She keeps inviting me over for dinner, and I'm running out of excuses. Maybe this Sunday. Another way to put the screws to Stu.

As for me, I'm still a bum. I'm thinking I might take over Hanky's place in society. I dunno, maybe, maybe not. Whatever. I spend a lot of time staring out across the expanse of Lake Superior apologizing to Stu for not shooting him, giving the guy a quicker and more comfortable death. I'd do it again, though. As for Ariel LaRioux and Kathleen Pierpont, enough has been said. I executed them and am only remorseful that I would never have a chance to do it again. They were terrible nasty people and deserved their fate. I find satisfaction that they are gone, but I'm sure there sure more like them lurking someplace.

Sy got another motorcycle, giving his house back to the ex-wife. I think he's following Bob Swearingen to Mexico.

I make sure that Rikki and Laura have well manicured grave sites and flowers on their birthdays. Nobody should be forgotten on their birthday. Mine is St. Patrick's day, in case you forgot.

Angie's brother had her remains sent to Wisconsin, getting her a spot in the family plot. Somebody loves her, and that's a good thing.

Jeanine is doing well, and we talk daily. She has some unsettled issues that keep most people at bay. Her relationship with the health club guy is tenuous, but she always was like that. I have a hunch that we aren't done yet as business partners.

And, I cry a lot. Too many good wonderful people have died, and I didn't. Someday. Someday I'll join them. Maybe I'll get shot by a jealous husband. So cool.

I spend a lot of time lamenting my life and the people who suffered for knowing me. Marci, Laura, Cheryl, Rikki, Angie, and yes, even Brew. All died senselessly, and I lived. I'm alive and they aren't. If there is a hell, I'm on its doorstep, waiting.

* *

If you ever get to the Duluth that's in Minnesota, stop in at Hell Burger and leave me a sticky note. Pin a ten dollar bill to it. I'm broke.

AUTHOR'S NOTE

● ●

W HEN YOU GO TO DULUTH AND VISIT THE charming Canal Park area, you won't find Hell Burger anymore. The doors were closed in October 2010. Mitch Omer and his beautiful wife, Cynthia Gerdes, are real and continue making a success of their on-going business, Hell's Kitchen, an iconic symbol in Minneapolis. Brian Melland is also very real, and is addicted to M&Ms. A bowl is kept in the Hell's Kitchen office to keep him satisfied. When you stop in, tell Mitch, Cynthia, or Brian, "Hello", from a fan. And, if you behave yourself, Mitch may sign the cookbook, *Damn Good Food*. Then take a trip to heaven in the Angel Food Bakery.

The other locations in Duluth are all real as well. The Leif Erickson Park Rose Garden is truly an impressive sight. One will see how appealing the garden was to Rikki and her father when she was a child. It was their church and held what they needed for spiritual comfort.

On the subject of the white slave trade, the upcoming mystery, *The Affair of Marci Hudson*, is the introduction to Norby Klein and his association with the often mentioned Marci, as one of the loves he laments over. White slavery does exist and is a frightening blight.

As you read the books I write, you will see that in some form or another, I delve into the subject of the mistreatment of women. It is a continuing war I wage on people who are compelled to abuse someone they are supposed to love. Please, stop the abuse.